"I don't need you to protect me," Jillian said.

"But you need me to get out of here." He let go of her for just a moment, so he could take a silk scarf from his pocket and wrap it around her eyes. He caught her wrists and bound those together, too.

"I thought you were letting me go."

"I am. I'm just not going to let you see where you've been." He couldn't trust that she wouldn't lead the police right back to him. As she fought against the scarves, he swung her up in his arms.

"How do I know you're really going to bring me out of here?" she asked, her voice trembling.

"You're going to have to trust me."

LISA CHILDS

MYSTERY LOVER

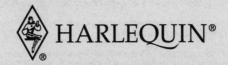

HARLEQUIN®

TORONTO • NEW YORK • LONDON
AMSTERDAM • PARIS • SYDNEY • HAMBURG
STOCKHOLM • ATHENS • TOKYO • MILAN • MADRID
PRAGUE • WARSAW • BUDAPEST • AUCKLAND

With eternal gratitude to Denise Zaza
for pulling my first Intrigue manuscript from the slush pile
eight years ago. I will never be able to thank you enough
for making my longtime dream of becoming
a published author a reality.

Recycling programs
for this product may
not exist in your area.

ISBN-13: 978-0-373-74534-0

MYSTERY LOVER

ABOUT THE AUTHOR

Bestselling, award-winning author Lisa Childs writes paranormal and contemporary romance for Harlequin and Silhouette Books. She lives on thirty acres in west Michigan with her husband, two daughters, a talkative Siamese and a long-haired Chihuahua who thinks she's a Rottweiler. Lisa loves hearing from readers who can contact her through her Web site, www.lisachilds.com, or snail mail address, P.O. Box 139, Marne, MI 49435.

Books by Lisa Childs

CAST OF CHARACTERS

Mystery Lover—His face masked, his identity unknown, he's referred to as a phantom. He's a man on a mission, who will allow nothing and no one to interfere with his plan. But he didn't plan on Jillian Drake and his attraction to her.

Jillian Drake—This ambitious reporter has discovered that the phantom is a flesh and blood man, and she'll do anything to uncover his identity. But she didn't intend to fall in love.

Tobias St. John—Is the powerful tycoon a victim, a villain or the imposter a little girl claims?

Tabitha St. John—The scared little girl needs help to prove the man who's claiming to be her father is really her kidnapper, and she implores Jillian to help not realizing she's risking the reporter's life.

Nick Morris—Tobias St. John's head of security, but is he the protector or the threat?

Mike Hanson—The producer wants Jillian for himself, but he's not above using her to get the story every network is after.

Chapter One

With a flash of fire, a spray of broken glass and an earsplitting boom, the world exploded behind Jillian Drake. Shattered glass might have lacerated her skin as flames burst from the building in front of which she'd been reporting, but strong arms had closed around her, lifting her off her feet and carrying her out of danger just seconds before the explosion.

Her heart hammered at her ribs beneath the heavily muscled arms that wound around her. She clutched at her protector's wool jacket, digging her fingers into the material to loosen his tight embrace. But his grip didn't ease until the heat from the fire receded into the damp night air and the brightness of the flames disappeared into darkness. Then the hold eased enough that Jillian slid down the hard length of his body until her feet touched the asphalt. She squirmed in those strong arms, turning toward the man who held her. But she couldn't see his face; she could see only the dark shadow of shoulders that seemed impossibly wide.

Her breath caught in her lungs, along with the scent of him: wood smoke, leather and something elementally male. She needed to thank him for saving her. But how had he known she would need saving? How had he known the building would explode?

"Who are you?" She asked the most important of all the questions swirling through her mind.

Releasing her completely, he dropped his arms from around her and stepped back. The sudden lack of warmth sent a chill racing through her. Where had he come from? Before the explosion, the area had been the scene of a break-in and was restricted to the police officers who'd been securing it. The police had arrived after the reporters, who were already filming in front of the building because it housed the executive offices of the most powerful and currently the most besieged man in Rapid City, Michigan.

She hadn't noticed her rescuer among the

uniforms and media, and standing only a few feet from him now, she could barely see his face. In the narrow alley between tall buildings, he appeared more shadow than human. Was he…?

No. It wasn't possible. Despite all the wild claims people had been making lately, there were no such thing as phantoms. He was real; Jillian had felt him, warm and strong, as he'd carried her off. To safety or danger? As well as the break-ins and explosions, there'd been a couple of murders, too, although no evidence had linked those crimes to these. To his?

"Who are you?" she asked again, tipping her head back as she tried to meet his gaze. She needed him to answer her, even if he didn't tell her his name; she needed to hear his voice, to know he could speak.

"Jillian!" someone urgently called for her. "Jillian!"

It was Charlie, her cameraman. God, what if he'd been hurt? She glanced back in the direction of the shouts and crackling noises of the fire. She had to check on her crew and make sure they were all right. She should have thought of them already.

She would have but for him. She turned

toward the man who'd rescued her. The darkness had swallowed him whole, revealing not even a glimmer of his eyes or an outline of those mammoth shoulders. All that remained of him was a faint, raspy-whispered threat. "Don't get too close."

So he could speak. She had questions she wanted to ask, but she couldn't when people she cared about were in danger. Ignoring him, she rushed back toward the burning building. "Charlie? Charlie?"

"Over here, Jillian," the curly-haired young man replied, heaving a sigh of relief as she ran up to where he shakily leaned against a car with a broken windshield. "Thank God you're okay," he told her. "I was filming you and then someone—or something—grabbed you. You were just gone. And then the building blew up…" He shuddered.

She reached out, knocking bits of glass and brick dust from his blond hair. Blood trickled from cuts on his face, dripping off his chin onto his T-shirt. "You're not okay. You're hurt."

"A lot less than you would have been if you'd been standing where you were…"

Jillian glanced back toward the building,

unable to discern, for all the debris, where she'd been standing on the sidewalk in front of it. Whoever had grabbed her had probably saved her life. "I'm fine," she assured Charlie. "And you will be, too. Help's coming."

Lights still flashed from the police cars that had already been at the scene when the building blew. Now other lights flashed and sirens blared as more fire engines and paramedics approached.

Charlie shook his head. "Hell's coming if we don't get some footage of this." But as he lifted the camera, his face contorted into a grimace of pain.

"You can't do this," she pointed out. "You're hurt."

"If we don't, we'll be dead. Mike'll kill us for not getting the story, especially with the national networks showing up to scoop us." He gestured toward the other reporters gathered around the burning building, already filming. "We're turning into a joke, not knowing what the hell's going on in our own city."

Anger surged through Jillian, heating her skin more than the flames licking up from the ruins of what had once been an office building. She remembered why she was out

here—past the curfew the mayor had declared
for River City, Michigan. For the past couple
of weeks, the city had been under siege, but
no one knew who had declared war or why.
Jillian was determined to find out, not just
because of the boost it would give her career,
but because she'd been ignorant once before
of what had been going on under her nose.
She wouldn't be that stupid—or trusting—
ever again.

"Where's Vicky?" she asked. "Please say
that she stayed in the van." The young assistant producer had been back in the vehicle,
checking the live feed to the station, when
the building had exploded and obliterated the
crime scene of broken windows and the front
door.

Charlie nodded. "She's okay. She was in
the van, which is parked far enough down the
street that it's out of the line of fire."

Just as Jillian had been—because of the
man from the shadows. But had he come from
the shadows or had he come from the fire like
Dante rising from his own inferno… Dante.
Maybe that was what she would have to call
him since he wouldn't tell her his name.

Vicky, her short dark hair mussed, pushed

through the police officers trying to secure the new perimeter of the crime scene. "God, Charlie, you're bleeding!"

With another grimace, he shrugged off her concern. "Help me with the camera. We have got to get some footage of the scene."

"We were rolling live when the explosion happened. We got some great stuff," Vicky assured them.

But it wasn't enough to capture what had happened; Jillian needed to know *why*. And apparently she wasn't the only one. Along with the police cars and the rescue crews that had rushed to the scene, a long, black limousine idled in the street.

"He's here," Jillian murmured, her pulse quickening with excitement as it always did in his proximity.

"It's his business that's burning down," Vicky said.

"They're all his businesses." Every one that had been broken into and burned down in the past two weeks had belonged to one man— the tycoon of River City, Tobias St. John. That was why so many camera crews had been filming outside his executive offices before the building had even exploded

She had no doubt that he knew what was going on and why, but she had no hope of getting him to share that information with her. Ever since she'd been hired by WXXM three years ago, she'd been trying to persuade Tobias St. John to grant her an interview— with no success. Even when they had run into each other during one of his rare public appearances, he'd only spoken one word to her.

No...

No...

The word reverberated inside his head like a shout, even though he hadn't uttered it aloud. He couldn't risk revealing his presence.

But he had risked everything—for her. He'd stepped out of the shadows. Hell, he'd run out of them to pull her to safety. Not that she had appreciated or stayed out of danger. She'd rushed right back into it.

The fire blazing behind her, she faced the camera. Her hair tangled around her face, the red waves nearly as vivid as those flames. Her green eyes focused on the lens as if she spoke to just one person, giving that one viewer her undivided attention. God, she was beautiful....

And so damn ambitious. And smart.

"Don't get too close," he warned her again. She wouldn't hear him this time since he hid again in the shadows. And if she had heard him the first time, she hadn't understood what he meant.

He hadn't been talking about the fire. He'd been talking about so much more. He couldn't let her get too close to the truth. Or she would destroy even more than the bomb he'd set inside the offices he'd robbed.

"CAN YOU GET THAT any clearer?" Jillian asked as she stared at herself on the monitor in the station control room. They wouldn't have had any footage at all if they hadn't been filming live from the scene, so they were able to play back what they'd broadcasted live. Her image blurred as the shadowy figure swept her off her feet. Squinting, she leaned closer to the screen, her hand on Vicky's thin shoulder. "Can you tell who he is?"

Vicky's breath shuddered out. "Don't you mean *what?* It has to be that monster all the witnesses you've interviewed keep talking about seeing at the crime scenes."

Jillian shook her head even as goose bumps lifted the skin on her arms, and the nape of her neck tingled. Those eyewitness accounts had been about as credible as campfire ghost stories. As if some phantom really rose from the sewers at night to attack the city...

She shrugged off her uneasiness the same way she always had when she pragmatically dismissed those stories told around the bonfire during summer camp. "Not possible."

"So you don't believe in monsters?" Vicky asked.

Jillian couldn't deny that there were monsters in the world. She'd interviewed a few over the years—in the form of serial killers and child abusers. And she'd lived with one.

"I know you don't believe that any of those people really saw anything, but..." Vicky pushed a button and another monitor brought up footage from a few days ago of an older woman speaking into the microphone Jillian held to her mouth.

"Can you tell us what you witnessed before the burglar alarm sounded at St. John's Fine Arts Store?" Jillian's voice emanated from the speakers as she posed the question to the witness.

"I don't know what it was that came out of the smashed windows at the front of the building," the older woman replied, her teeth clattering together as she trembled. "It was so big—like some kind of giant—dressed all in black."

"Did you see his face?" Jillian asked. "Could you identify him?"

"I don't even know if it was a man," the woman replied. "He didn't have a face."

More monitors on the wall of the editing room flickered to life—with footage of other interviews, other witnesses saying the same things.

"It was huge."

"Scary."

"Something out of this world—a monster."

"It was a ghost."

"A phantom."

"It wasn't human. It couldn't have been…."

Jillian focused on just one of those monitors, the one that showed her being lifted in the arms of the man everyone else called a monster. And she called her rescuer.

Charlie had had the camera trained on her as she reported about the attacks on Tobias St. John's businesses, including the robbery in progress at his executive offices. When the man, who was so tall, grabbed her, his head didn't enter the frame. The screen showed only the long, muscular body and broad shoulders, but no face.

"So what was it?" Vicky asked. "You got closer than any of these other witnesses."

Don't get too close...

Had he been talking about the burning building...or himself?

Jillian uttered a shuddery sigh of frustration. "I don't know. The building had just exploded. I was in the dark with him. And distracted. Charlie started calling out for me. I had to make sure he was all right and that you were okay, too."

Vicky flinched. "It was so scary even just watching from the van. I saw that *thing* grab you and then everything blew up. The lens shattered and the camera broke." Her young voice cracked as she relived the terror. "I didn't know what had happened to you or to Charlie."

"I wasn't sure, either," Jillian admitted. "It all took place so quickly."

"But he let you go," Vicky said. "He saved you instead of killing you…like he probably killed those other women."

Jillian shivered. "We don't know that he's responsible for those murders." Two young women had died, the first just over two weeks ago. The body of the second had been found recently, but she'd probably died around the same time as the first victim, according to the coroner. "They died before people started talking about seeing this…"

"Monster," Vicky said. "But their deaths have to be related. The first woman was the nanny of Tobias St. John's little girl."

Not only had his businesses been attacked, but his nanny had been killed. Fortunately his daughter hadn't been with her; the woman had been alone in the park. His daughter must have been home with him. According to Jillian's sources, her mother had divorced Tobias and left years ago.

"You're lucky to be alive," Vicky cautioned her.

"If he'd wanted me dead, he would have

just left me standing in front of that building, and the explosion would have done the job for him."

"Like it could have killed Charlie." Vicky rubbed at her eyes, as if dashing away tears. She cared about the cameraman, but she wouldn't admit to having feelings for a co-worker. "I'm glad you sent him home. He really got hurt."

Jillian nodded. "I hope he went to the emergency room." She winced over a twinge of guilt. Even though he'd insisted he was fine, she should have driven him to the hospital. But she'd taken his word instead because she'd wanted to see the footage of the explosion, had wanted to see what she'd missed.

"He won't be able to get to the E.R. now—with the citywide curfew," Vicky reminded her.

"The hospital won't shut down." Even though most of the city closed early in order to comply with the mayor's order. But was it the mayor's or was it Tobias St. John's? He was the one who had the most to lose. He'd almost single-handedly turned River City from a small town into a thriving metropolis. Although with the way his businesses had been attacked the past couple of weeks, he had considerably less than he once had.

"How are you getting home?" Vicky asked. "The subway and the buses aren't running anymore."

"I have my car." But she wasn't driving home. Not yet. "I'd take you, but I'm going to stick around here for a little while."

"You won't be able to leave, anyway," Vicky reminded her. "The police have most of the roads barricaded."

"Not that it's done any good stopping him," Jillian remarked.

"'Course not." The young producer snorted in derision. "Curfews and roadblocks aren't going to affect him. He's a phantom."

"He's real." No ghost could have carried her like that—muscular arms tight around her, beneath the swell of her breasts, where her heart had pounded wildly with shock…and fear. But Dante, as she'd decided to call him, hadn't harmed her; he'd saved her.

"That's not what the witnesses claim." Vicky pointed toward all those monitors.

"These are the same people who march outside the station with their picket signs proclaiming that Armageddon's coming. The end is near," she said, dismissing them.

"Tonight, when that building exploded, didn't you think they were right?" the younger woman asked. "I did. And whatever the hell he is, he gives me nightmares." Vicky shuddered as she rose from her chair. "But I'm going to try to get some sleep, anyway. There's a couch with my name on it in the break room. You can use the one in Mike's office."

Jillian shook her head, her focus on that one monitor with the dark blur behind her. Had he been just a shadow? Just a figment of her imagination? No. She could still feel those arms around her, his breath on her neck. "I'm not tired."

"Mike'll want you to get your beauty rest," Vicky teased her.

"Mike wants too much," she murmured, thinking of their lecherous producer. Some of her coworkers thought she'd been given her job because of her looks rather than her talent. While she wanted to prove them wrong, she was the one to whom she had the most to prove. She'd failed herself tonight. She'd been close, physically close, to her first real lead. And she'd run away from him.

Tears of frustration stung her eyes, but she blinked them back to focus again on that shadow. Nothing would distract her from her goal again—not anyone else's safety. Not even her own.

RAGE COURSED THROUGH St. John with such heat that it felt as if he was burning from the inside out. The son of a bitch had struck again. Had he no respect for the rules of their agreement, for *him?* He was the powerful one. Hadn't he already proved that?

Trembling with an all-consuming anger, he flung open the door to his den and strode across the hardwood floor to the bar in the corner of it. A drink might calm his temper for now. Only one thing would settle it for good, though.

Two of the guards who'd ridden with him to the site of the latest destruction hovered just inside the door. They exchanged a look. Then one of them cleared his throat and said, "I don't understand why the offices were attacked."

It was personal; that was the reason for the attack. Didn't these idiots understand that? But then how could they when there was so much they didn't know? Only one other person knew everything.

"What about the house?" he asked. "Was there a security breach here?"

One of the guards stepped inside the den. "No."

Why not? What game was he playing?

"There is something you need to see, though," the guard said, clicking on the plasma TV over the fireplace. "This played out live earlier, and Morris recorded it for you to see."

St. John expected security footage; instead, he watched a news broadcast. A reporter had been standing in front of the building before it had exploded.

"What am I watching?" he asked the guard. He already knew what had happened to that building. And why.

"You'll see…"

He studied the woman's image on the flat screen. With her pale skin and bright eyes, she illuminated the dark room. Until the shadow swallowed her up and stole away with her. Then flames burst out of the building, shattering the lens. But the tape began again, seconds later—with a new lens and a disheveled reporter. However, more than mere seconds had passed before her reappearance.

"Did you see it?" the guard asked. "Someone, or *something,* saved her from the explosion."

"Who is she?" St. John asked.

The guard's brow furrowed with surprise. "Uh, Jillian Drake. She's been hassling you for years to grant her an interview."

He nodded, but didn't really remember her. Maybe it was time that he talked to her. Only, she'd be the one answering the questions. He leaned closer to the screen and studied her beautiful face and those unfathomable eyes. What had she learned?

How much did she know?

Enough to get her killed?

Chapter Two

Biceps bulging with the weight of the automatic weapons they carried, guards paced back and forth behind the wrought-iron gate. When Jillian stepped from her car, they turned toward her, their gun barrels pointed directly at her.

"Get back in your vehicle, Ms. Drake," they ordered.

She wasn't the only one who'd been warned away. But she was the only one who hadn't listened. The other reporters had moved behind the guarded perimeter of the estate, just as they had the previous evening when they had avoided the danger of the exploding building…and the faceless man.

"I'm not leaving until I talk to Mr. St. John," she insisted. This time she was not going to take no for an answer.

But was he even home? She couldn't see much beyond the gates. She hadn't been able to even before night had begun to fall. The house sat far back on the winding drive. A high, cement wall, ancient trees and thorny shrubs shielded it from the street. It was as if the home inhabited its own land—remote and impenetrable. Even the air around it felt otherworldly; the sky seemed darker and hung low, close to the treetops.

The wind whipped through the branches and slapped her long hair across her face. "Let me in," she persisted.

"You're trespassing," one of the guards, a burly blond giant, warned her.

She lifted her chin and stared down the gun barrels trained on her. "I'm not leaving." They hadn't called the police to haul her away, nor had they shot her. Yet. "I just want to talk to him. I didn't bring a camera crew with me." As had the others who filmed from across the street.

"You're still not getting inside," the same guard informed her. She recognized him from the other times she had camped outside the gates, trying to get the billionaire to grant her an interview. But then the blond guard had been alone; now there were several other men guarding the gates and pacing the perimeter of the estate. "You know St. John's rules. The press is not allowed inside. No exceptions."

"Because of his daughter?" she asked, calling up the excuse he'd previously used to avoid interviews. The girl's nanny hadn't been killed at the estate, but her death implied that everyone close to him was in danger. And no one was closer than his daughter. Of course he'd added extra security. "Or because he's scared?"

One of the guards laughed while the rest made some pithy comments. But then the engine of an approaching vehicle drowned out their voices. A long, black car drew up next to her small sedan, so close the side mirrors nearly touched. The high beam of its bright lights blinded her. She lowered her head and squinted, trying to see beyond the light and the tinted windows. Behind her the metal gates shuddered as they opened.

She didn't need to see inside the car to know who occupied it—*Tobias St. John*. She was not going to let him get away with denying her an interview this time—not when she suspected he was one of the few who knew why

River City was under siege. While the police department might have been too intimidated to force him to answer all their questions, she was not.

She turned toward the opening gates and ran through them. But strong hands caught her arms, jerking her to a stop as the car continued past her. She reached out, straining to break free of the guard's grasp, and pounded against the side of the limousine. "Stop! Stop!"

To her surprise, the long car lurched to a halt halfway through the gate. The rear side window slid down and a deep voice rumbled, "Let her go."

The guard dropped his hand from her arm, which burned from his tight grip, and she stumbled forward, falling against the car. She'd left her coat in her sedan and wore only a thin silk blouse, which the cool spring wind chilled. Trembling, she leaned over and peered into the dim interior of the limo.

St. John was not much more than a hulking shadow with broad shoulders and chest in a dark suit. Only his light-colored eyes glittered in the shadows. "Miss Drake, I take it you want to speak with me?"

The ominous tone of his voice had her

swallowing down a lump of fear before replying, "Yes."

The door pushed Jillian back as he opened it and ordered, "Get in."

Her heart rose to her throat with a rush of relief and trepidation. "Thank you," she murmured as she scrambled inside the car and settled onto the leather seat across from him.

"Don't thank me yet," he said, his voice deep with warning.

She shivered, uneasy over his ominous tone. "Mr. St. John, I want to ask you…"

Before she could finish her question, the car stopped again—at the front door to the mansion. Floodlights illuminated the dark exterior, which appeared to be either slate or granite. Had the home been carved from rock? Had the man? He didn't move until the chauffeur opened the door and helped her from the back. Then in one lithe moment, he stepped onto the sidewalk beside her.

"Let's talk inside, Miss Drake," he said, his hand on her back guiding her toward the front door. Two guards with automatic weapons stood sentry. Were they keeping people out or *in?*

Goose bumps rose on her skin, his touch chilling her to the bone despite the warmth of his skin penetrating the thin silk of her blouse. Ordinarily she would have fired question after question at him, taking advantage of the opportunity to finally speak personally to the man. But his easy acquiescence unsettled her.

"I appreciate that you're a busy man," she said, resisting the urge to shrug off his hand. "So I won't take up too much of your time."

"Then why did you insist on seeing me?" he asked, gesturing for her to pass in front of him as the guards opened the door for them.

"A better question might be why you finally agreed to see me," she said. She wasn't the only reporter he'd refused to be interviewed by over the years; St. John was a notorious publicity-phobe.

He laughed a deep rumble of a chuckle. "You're so suspicious, Miss Drake."

Jillian nearly laughed now. In the past, she hadn't been suspicious enough, and she had learned a painful lesson. One she didn't need repeated. She noticed bars on the windows, and an irrational fear overcame her that if she stepped inside, she might never be allowed to leave again.

"Miss Drake?" he prompted her as she hesitated outside the door. "What's the problem?"

That was what she intended to find out. She drew in a quick breath and walked across the threshold. "No problem," she said. "I'm just not used to you letting me inside."

He chuckled, and like his earlier warning, it had the same ominous tone. "You're not quite inside yet."

She stood in the foyer on black marble flooring, which sparkled in the light of a crystal chandelier that hung overhead.

He turned back toward her, and the light bathed his face. Despite his aversion to the media, he'd been photographed several times—at charity events, ribbon-cutting ceremonies, et cetera. Jillian had pored over those photos as if they would tell her the secrets the powerful man had refused to share with her—or anyone else. She had known he was tall; anyone who'd ever met him always remarked on what a big man he was. Larger than life. Magnetic.

Until tonight, Jillian had been drawn to

him, too, but now she hesitated again when he gestured for her to precede him through the foyer. She studied his face, the sharp nose, the heavy jaw and those arrestingly pale blue eyes. "Thank you for letting me in…."

His bright gaze traveled from the top of her head to the pointy toes of her high-heeled pumps. "I can't imagine why I never did before."

"You didn't want to be interviewed," she reminded him as a chill chased across her skin, along with the feeling that he had undressed her with that thorough inspection. She suppressed a shiver at her overreaction.

In the past, when she'd gotten close enough to exchange a glance or request an interview, she'd been attracted to his good looks. Maybe she preferred when he'd played hard to get. Or maybe being caught up in murder and mayhem had cooled her interest in him.

His lips curved into a grin. "An interview would be a waste of your time, Miss Drake. I learned long ago how to keep my secrets."

"I know." She'd had to dig deep to find out the little she had about him: he'd divorced over irreconcilable differences and his ex-wife had exchanged custody of their daughter for a very generous settlement. Had Tobias ever met anyone he hadn't been able to buy off or intimidate?

His gaze held hers with an intensity that belied the grin playing around his hard-looking mouth. "But I don't think it would be a waste of my time for me to learn *your* secrets."

After three years of mostly ignoring her, except when she'd gotten in his face at charity events, now he flirted with her? He was nearly as confusing as the man everyone claimed was a phantom.

"I have no secrets, Mr. St. John," she claimed. At least, none that anyone had cared enough to discover. The reporter reported the story; she wasn't the story. Maybe that was why she had chosen the career that she had.

"Every woman has her secrets," St. John said, stepping closer to her so that she felt the heat of his breath as well as his muscular body. "Like who you're seeing…"

She resisted the urge to shudder and bit her lip, hoping he wouldn't physically touch her now when in the past she'd yearned for it. "What makes you think I'm seeing some-one?" She had hardly dated since her divorce, but her single status wasn't something she cared to share with Tobias St. John.

"I saw him last night," he said, "on the news, saving you from that explosion."

She shook her head. "That—that wasn't my boyfriend."

"Then who is he?" St. John asked, his blue eyes narrowed with more than mere curiosity.

"I was hoping you could tell me," she admitted. "That's why I had to talk to you."

His grin faded, and his gaze hardened even more. "You want me to introduce you to him?"

Her rescuer hadn't been willing to introduce himself, even though she'd asked for his name. Twice. Regardless of the nickname she'd given him, she needed his real identity. "So you do know who he is…"

He shook his head.

"But you must have some idea," she persisted, "if he's the one responsible for the damage to all your businesses." And the murders of the nanny and the other young woman who had yet to be identified. Had Dante been responsible for those, too?

St. John touched her now, his big hand

wrapping around her arm in a grip that had her wincing. "Do you know that he's responsible?"

"I have no proof," she admitted. But she'd spent a sleepless night trying to figure it out. He wouldn't have known the building was going to explode unless he had been the one who'd set the charges. "But it could be him…"

"It could be any number of other people," St. John pointed out. "A man doesn't achieve all the success that I have without making some enemies."

"That's true," she agreed as she pulled a file from the side pocket of her briefcase-style purse and flipped open to the list she'd compiled. "I found them—men who think you shafted them in business deals. Women hurt when you reneged on commitments." She'd found past lovers, but not his ex-wife. That woman had left the country shortly after their divorce. Unwilling or afraid to stay on the same continent with him?

He chuckled as he glanced at the contents of the file. "Your research is very thorough."

"That's why my reports are always so accurate. I'm damn good at my job," she told him, hoping he would finally take her seriously. He never had in the past, as he'd either refused her calls or walked away from her with just that one word. But even though he'd told her no every time, he'd had a certain look in his eyes—a certain intensity when he stared her down that suggested he might have been willing to say yes to something else. Her attraction hadn't been entirely one-sided.

But now that she'd spent more than a few minutes in his company, she realized she'd been attracted to the myth more than the man. An ex-marine who'd become a billionaire, Tobias St. John had impressed her with his ingenuity and drive. But he was just a man.

"Then you must realize that any one of these people—" he waved the file he'd taken from her "—could be behind the attacks on my businesses."

She shook her head, rejecting the list of suspects she'd compiled. "None of them match the description of the man who witnesses have placed at the scene of every attack on your business."

"Man?" he asked doubtfully. Obviously he'd heard the same witness reports that she had.

"You think he's a phantom or a monster?" she asked.

"Gun for hire, monster—same difference," he said, dismissing her rescuer.

"So you think that someone hired him to sabotage your businesses?" she asked.

"You've done the research," he reminded her, tapping his finger against the folder he had yet to return to her. "Don't you think so, too?"

No. The mysterious stranger hadn't given her the impression that he was the type of man who took orders from anyone else.

St. John must have sensed her hesitation because he narrowed his eyes. "You don't think so. What do you know, Miss Drake, that you haven't shared with the public?"

"I'm the one who's supposed to ask the questions," she reminded him. "Why don't you increase security at your businesses instead of just increasing it here at the estate?"

"How I conduct my business is none of yours, Miss Drake," he warned her, his eyes darkening with anger.

"You must have increased security at the estate to protect your daughter," she pushed.

A bone clicked as he clenched his jaw. "Miss Drake…"

"Do you think this man might also be responsible for the death of your daughter's nanny?" She finally asked what she'd considered the most important question of all, and the one she'd suspected he was least likely to answer. He'd absolutely refused to reply to any inquiries about his daughter in the past, determined to protect her from the public.

"I didn't let you in here for an interview," he said, his voice so cold that she couldn't suppress a shiver this time. "I let you in here so I could get some answers. And you are going to tell me what I want to know."

She shook her head. "I don't know anything about that man…" Except that he had saved her life last night.

St. John tensed and tilted his head, then touched the earpiece she hadn't previously noticed that he wore. "You are going to tell me what you do know," he said, "but first you'll have to excuse me."

"That's fine," she replied with a slight step back. "I'll just show myself out."

"You're not going anywhere just yet, Miss Drake," he said with a glance toward the guards who stood near the front door. "Not until we talk."

She shook her head and eased another step away. "No…"

"Help yourself to a drink." He gestured toward the bar that lined one wall of the living room. "I'll be back shortly."

"I won't be here," she murmured after he disappeared down the hall—with her file. If he'd hoped to slow down her investigation, his effort was pointless. She had copies of all her research. She walked from the living room into the marble foyer, but the guards— the blond man from the gate and another guy with a buzz cut that suggested he was ex-military—lifted their weapons toward her again. Anger and panic had blood racing through her veins. "You can't keep me here."

"You wanted inside the gates, Ms. Drake," the blond reminded her.

She had wanted in, but except for that brief, irrational flash of fear, she hadn't seriously thought that she wouldn't be allowed to leave again.

"Son of a bitch," he murmured as he fumbled with connecting the wires to the charges.

He stretched out his gloved hands, forcing them to steady. He needed to focus on what he was doing—not on her.

He hadn't allowed himself to be distracted before. Not with the enormity of what was at stake…

But Jillian Drake's beautiful face haunted him, her eyes so full of curiosity, intelligence and determination. She wouldn't stop until she either found out what was going on or got herself killed. Hell, finding out what was going on was certain to get her killed.

But it wasn't just her life she risked with her prying.

The wires connected, he headed for the exit. But, still distracted, he didn't move fast enough to clear the building before the first charge exploded.

Chapter Three

Jillian peered down the hall in the direction Tobias St. John had rushed off. A thin beam of light, and an angry murmur, emanated from under the closed door of what she presumed was his home office.

Something's happening...

And instead of being out there reporting it, she was stuck inside St. John's compound—missing it. Her hand shook with frustration... and fear...as she reached inside her purse for her cell.

Metal clinked as a gun shifted. "Ms. Drake." One of the guards spoke her name as a warning.

"I have to check my phone," she said. But when she glanced at the LCD screen, the cell indicated no signal. What the hell...? She whirled toward the closest guard, that blond-haired giant. "Does St. John have some special device that blocks cell phones from receiving or transmitting calls?"

A smirk curling his lip, the guy chuckled. "Maybe you didn't pay for your service."

"I need to use a phone," she said, careful to inject only impatience and none of her fear into her voice.

The guy just chuckled again and shook his head.

"C'mon, I need to make a call," she implored him. She needed to get the hell out of there.

"You planning on calling the police?" the other guard goaded her, as if she didn't already know River City's finest answered more to St. John than their chief.

Who was to say that the nanny had really died at the park and not the estate? St. John? The authorities who'd believe whatever he told them in exchange for another *donation?*

"I have to check in with my producer," she said, which was actually the truth. "I'm late for work."

"Maybe you should have thought about that before you ran through the gates," the blond guy said with that aggravating smirk.

"My producer knows I'm here," she warned them with a lie this time. "He knows I'm working on a story about St. John." That much was true. And she was convinced, from the raised voice booming through that closed door, that something else had happened that she needed to be reporting.

Then the door opened with such force that it slammed against the wall. "Bring the damn car around!" St. John bellowed at the guards.

The two burly men nearly knocked heads together in their urgency to run for the door. Self-preservation compelled Jillian to follow them, but she'd disregarded that instinct before when she'd been chasing down a story. And she'd survived…

"What's going on?" she asked instead. "What's happened?"

St. John's eyes gleamed with an anger so intense it almost bordered on madness. He shook his head.

"I'm going to find out," she persisted. "You might as well tell me."

As if he hadn't heard her at all, he headed toward the door the men had left open behind them. Rubber screeched as the long black limo pulled up to the sidewalk.

Rushing after him, she grabbed at the sleeve of his suit jacket and implored, "Let me go with you!"

St. John caught her hand in his, his grasp so tight she winced in pain. "I'm sorry, Miss Drake, but that's not possible."

"We can talk," she said. "I'll tell you what I've found out about that man—the one everyone's been seeing at the crime scenes."

His lips curved into a grin. "There's nothing to talk about anymore."

"What—what do you mean?"

"He might have gotten you out of harm's way last night—" St. John chuckled "—but he didn't get himself out of it tonight."

"There was another explosion?"

He nodded, and anger flashed in his eyes again before the grin reappeared. "And there's a body…"

Her heart kicked against her ribs. "His?"

St. John's broad shoulders lifted in a slight shrug, but his eyes gleamed with satisfaction.

"Let me go with you!" she insisted, anxious to get to the scene and learn the truth.

"It's over, Miss Drake. There is no story," he said, leaving her standing in the foyer as he stepped inside the limo and slammed the door.

The attacks on his businesses might have ended tonight, but the story was still out there, waiting for Jillian to break it. She stepped over the threshold to follow the car that was pulling away, but something tugged at her skirt, holding her back. She glanced down into the bright eyes of a dark-haired little girl.

Just as she had that file on all of St. John's enemies, Jillian had compiled information on every aspect of his life, including his family. Of course, that hadn't taken long as the only family he had was his daughter.

"Hello, Tabitha," she greeted the child as she crouched to her level.

"You're that lady," the little girl exclaimed, "the one my daddy watches on TV."

"Uh, yes," she replied, surprised that St. John actually watched her special reports. "My name is Jillian Drake."

"Jilly," the child murmured.

A smile curved her lips, and she nodded. "Your daddy had to leave," she explained, glancing around to see if the new nanny had followed the child down the stairs from her bedroom. Tobias couldn't have run out without a thought to his daughter's well-being. St. John was notoriously overprotective of his child. But of course he thought the threat to her safety was gone, so he probably hadn't given orders to the guards to stand sentry at her bedroom door. Instead they'd left with him.

The little girl shook her head, tumbling her tangled curls around her thin shoulders. She trembled as the cold breeze blew through the open door and hit her thin cotton nightgown. Her fingers still knotted in the fabric of Jillian's skirt, she tugged again until Jillian leaned closer.

"Can I tell you a secret?" the child asked, her blue eyes solemn. Had she not realized that her father watched Jillian every night because she was on the news? At five years old, Tabitha St. John was undoubtedly too young to understand what a reporter did and who Jillian was.

But Jillian found herself nodding in reply. After all, what kind of secret would a child want her to keep? The fact that she was up past her bedtime? "You can tell me anything," she offered.

Tabitha pitched her voice to a breathy whisper and shared, "That man is not my daddy."

"What man?" Jillian asked, wondering if the child had a male nanny.

"That man that just left…the one who looks like my daddy…" The child shuddered. "He's not my daddy."

Blood. So much damn blood…

The man—or monster some people believed he was—couldn't figure out what blood belonged to him and what to someone else. He stared down at the streaks of it on his gloves and covering his torn jeans and coat. His guts twisted with pain and guilt over the senseless loss of a good man.

This was his damn war. If there were any casualties, it should have been him. Not someone who'd only been trying to help in the battle to bring down St. John.

Once again in the familiar shadows his existence had become, he leaned against a brick wall and stared down the narrow alley to where the building behind him burned, smoke and flames rising from it. His mind flashed back to the night before, to when he'd carried Jillian Drake to safety. If he hadn't grabbed her when he had, he might have had her blood on his hands, too.

Hell, he still might. She wasn't about to give up trying to figure out what was going on in River City.

Sirens wailed in the distance, but help came too late. For his friend. And maybe for him…

But he couldn't give up now. Not yet. Not with so much riding on his winning this war. He sucked in a breath, ignoring the piercing pain in his ribs, and eased away from the wall. He had to keep walking…had to increase the distance between himself and the burning building and all that blood.

JILLIAN DROPPED to her knees so that she could peer directly into the eyes of the solemn child. "Honey, what do you mean?"

The little girl shuddered. "He's not my daddy."

"Why would you think such a thing?" Jillian asked in surprise. She'd thought herself the only one who, as a child, had wished her father wasn't her father. "Did you just have a bad dream?"

Tabitha shook her head. "It's not a dream." Her bottom lip trembled as tears welled in her eyes. "I—I wish it was. Then I could wake up."

Jillian had no experience with children. Instead of babysitting, she'd had a paper route, which she'd kept as she'd gotten older and worked on the school paper. But some instinct she didn't know she possessed compelled her to wrap her arms around the child's shaking shoulders. "It's okay, honey. It's okay…"

Tabitha buried her face in Jillian's hair and sniffled. "No, it's not. I want my daddy…" Her quiet voice rose with a cry that squeezed Jillian's heart.

She pulled the child away so that she could study her delicate, tearstained face. "I still don't understand, sweetheart. Why do you think Tobias isn't your father?"

Her bottom lip trembled again. "He just isn't…"

"Tabitha! Why aren't you in bed?" a female voice, pitched to shrillness, demanded. "You're not supposed to be down here."

Jillian glanced up to the blond-haired woman standing on the stairs. "I'm—"

"Yeah, I know who you are," the woman said as she ran down the last of the steps, grabbed Tabitha's shoulders and pulled the little girl away from Jillian. "What are you doing here?"

Jillian rose to her feet and reassured the anxious woman. "It's okay that I'm here. Mr. St. John let me in."

"He's gone now," the woman pointed out. "And you should be gone, too."

"Who are you?" Jillian asked, wondering at the identity of the young woman who St. John had taken the time to tell he was leaving, apparently via telephone or intercom, before he'd rushed off.

"That's not any of your business," the woman replied.

"My *new* nanny," Tabitha murmured, her eyes narrowed in a glare as she glanced up at the woman. "Susan…"

Jillian could understand the woman's anxiety, given that her predecessor had been murdered. But her reporter's instincts had her suspecting that there was more to Susan's unease than another woman's death.

The blonde squeezed the little girl's shoulders, then turned her around and steered her toward the stairs. "Get back to bed," she ordered.

"I want to talk to Jilly," Tabitha protested.

"Get to bed now!"

The child and Jillian both winced at the volume and the tone of the woman's angry command. "You don't have to yell at her," Jillian protested. For a brief moment she slipped into her own past—with all the angry voices echoing inside her head. "Please don't yell at her."

"Now!" Susan said, with another shove at Tabitha's back. The child stumbled up the steps.

"Don't be so rough with her," Jillian said. While she had no experience caring for kids, she had experience being one—one who'd been yelled at and shoved around her whole childhood. "I'll report you to Mr. St. John," she warned the woman. Despite his reputation as a ruthless businessman, he'd always been described as a patient, loving father. He must have been too busy with the business attacks to realize that the new nanny was not working out. "I'll tell him how you're treating his daughter."

A smug smile curved the woman's lips. "He's aware that she's become a problem."

Jillian flinched. "A problem?" That was how her father had described her, too—as a problem, a mistake, as someone who'd always been in his way....

"She's a difficult kid," Susan explained. "She needs a firm hand. It appears you need one, too."

"I want to make sure Tabitha's all right. She just recently lost her longtime nanny. You should be more sensitive with her." Jillian didn't have to be an expert on children to understand that.

"You talked to her for a few seconds. You have no idea what's going on with her or what she needs right now," the woman replied.

"True," Jillian admitted with a slight sigh. "I have no idea..." The girl's claim had confused the hell out of her.

"What? Was she spouting that nonsense about her father not being her father?" the woman asked with a derisive snort.

Jillian had learned long ago to never reveal a source. She just lifted her shoulders in a shrug. "Why would a little girl say something like that?"

Unless the claims about what kind of father St. John was were as inaccurate as those eye-witness reports describing the man with no face as a phantom...

"Because she's a spoiled brat," Susan replied with disgust now. "Daddy is a little too busy dealing with the coward who's going after his businesses to give her his undivided attention for once, so she's acting out."

"Really?" Jillian persisted.

The woman glared at her now. "You know what's been going on. You've been reporting the break-ins and explosions. You know someone's going after him."

Jillian nodded. "Of course I know that. Do you have any idea who this...*coward* is?" She wouldn't have referred to anyone brave enough to take on Tobias St. John as a coward.

Susan pursed her lips and shook her head, tumbling bleached-blond hair around her thin shoulders. "I don't know anything about his business."

"You're really just the nanny?" she asked. The woman seemed more familiar with St. John than an employee who'd only been working for him for a couple of weeks would.

That smug smile curving her lips again, Susan just nodded in reply.

"So you'd be the expert on children," Jillian prodded the blonde, who nodded again. "I guess I know nothing about kids because denying her father seems an unusual way for a five-year-old to act out."

"You know nothing about Tabitha St. John," the woman reminded her. "She's a smart little girl, precocious even. She knows how to cause trouble. Are you?"

"Am I what?" Jillian asked.

The woman stepped closer to her, as if threatening Jillian, even though she was shorter and slighter. "Are you going to cause trouble?"

"I don't know what you mean," she lied. Hell, ever since she was a kid, she'd been referred to as a troublemaker—because she found out the things people would rather no one else knew. But she'd missed some things over the years, things she should have noticed.

"Are you going to cause trouble for Mr.

St. John?" Susan repeated. "Are you going to report that nonsense his daughter told you?"

"I never report anything I can't prove," Jillian assured her.

"Then you're an unusual reporter."

"Working for Mr. St. John these past two weeks, you must have come to expect the unusual," Jillian said. "After what happened to his last nanny, aren't you afraid?"

Susan shook her head. "The estate is well-protected. No one's going to get on the grounds without his permission. He'll make certain of that."

Jillian nodded. "You seem to know him pretty well. Do you know why someone's attacking his business?"

The woman shrugged. "Jealousy? Greed? Mr. St. John is a powerful man. Every man wants to be him." Her brown eyes narrowed with another threat. "Every woman wants to be with him."

Jillian barely resisted the urge to shudder again as the woman obviously warned her away from seducing the man. "Are you more than his employee?"

"What I am is none of your business, Miss Drake. You better leave." The woman's breath caught with a gasp of fear. "You won't want Mr. St. John to return and find out that you're still poking around."

While Susan was obviously involved with her employer, she also feared him. Just as his daughter did.

"See Miss Drake to her car," the woman said, gesturing toward the guards who'd just walked in the open door. She must have summoned them.

But when? When she'd noticed the child gone from her bed or when she'd seen Jillian talking to Tabitha?

Jillian shook her head, trying to clear it of the notion the little girl had put there. The nanny wouldn't have needed muscle to track down a child missing from her bed. She'd only wanted to get rid of the reporter. Jillian was used to that; she wasn't used to dealing with children and their overactive imaginations.

Of course, Tobias was really the little girl's father. The man looked exactly as he had on those few occasions over the years when she'd gotten close to him. He also looked like all those photos Jillian had collected of him for her research. And he had no family but his daughter. Who else could he be?

"I'm leaving," Jillian assured all of St. John's employees. But as she backed toward the door, she glanced up the stairs, to where the little girl stood on the landing.

The child mouthed the words, *Help me...*

Chapter Four

"Where the hell were you?" Mike Hanson demanded. "All hell's breaking loose in the city and you're not answering your damn phone! If the public didn't love you, I'd fire your ass right now."

Jillian flinched at the shouting coming through her earpiece. Then she forced a smile as Charlie turned on the camera. "Jillian Drake reporting from the scene of the latest attack on River City. Unlike previous incidents, tonight there was a fatality in the explosion that followed the break-in at St. John's Jewelry Shoppe. Police have yet to identify the body, but from the size of the man they found, they believe him to be the suspect responsible for the reign of terror that's plagued our city over the past two weeks."

While she held on to her broadcaster's

expressionless face, her heart contracted with regret. Just last night he had saved her life— only to lose his twenty-four hours later. At least now the wild stories would stop. Despite the claims, he was mortal; he'd died in one of the explosions he'd undoubtedly set.

But what about those women? Had he been responsible for their deaths, too? If he'd killed them, why hadn't he killed her, too?

"However, the mayor has refused to rescind the city's curfew until the suspect's identity is confirmed. Please stay tuned to WXXM, Channel 13, for more information as it becomes available." She hung on to a smile until Charlie indicated he'd shut off the camera.

"Let's get down to the morgue to see if the coroner knows anything yet," she said. She'd arrived at the burning building just as the body bag had been loaded into the back of the van. As she'd reported, the man had been huge; three morgue attendants had had to lift the stretcher on which he lay. With the bag zipped, she hadn't been able to see the body, but one of the attendants had remarked that he hadn't had a face.

Just like the man who'd pulled her from danger the night before. Except he must have had a face; she just hadn't seen it. The dead man's face—whatever it had been—was gone now, burned by the explosion, according to one of the coroner's assistants.

"Want to ride in the van with me and Vicky?" Charlie asked as he loaded his equipment into the back of it.

She shook her head. "I brought my car. I better drive myself."

"Remember the curfew hasn't been lifted. The police might not let you through the barricades," Vicky warned her as she hurried to help Charlie. In addition to the cuts on his face, he'd bruised some ribs in the explosion the night before.

"I doubt that they're going to enforce the curfew tonight. They think the reign of terror is over." Tobias St. John did; that was why he'd left her alone in his fortress. Jillian's instincts warned her otherwise.

"You don't?" Charlie asked.

She shrugged. "Only time will tell."

"It's late," Vicky said with a fearful glance at the night sky. "You really should ride with us."

And feel like a third wheel as the assistant producer gazed adoringly at the cameraman?

"No, I'll be fine. I can take care of myself."
She'd been doing it for a long time now.

Jillian handed back the earpiece and the
mike. "I'll meet you two at the morgue."

Vicky shuddered. "That doesn't sound very
reassuring."

"Really, I'll be fine. You need to go down
there and get set up before those national networks steal all the good spots. This is our
city and our damn story." She slammed the
door shut and pounded on the side of the van,
waving them off.

Even if they didn't get stopped at police
barricades, they probably wouldn't get close
to the morgue. All the other crews had already left, leaving the scene deserted but for
the yellow crime-scene tape and the tendrils
of smoke rising from the debris into the dark
night sky. The force of the explosion had
broken the streetlamps so that Jillian had only
the faint glow from stars high overhead to
guide her way back to her car. Glass ground
beneath the heels of her shoes as she hurried
down the street to where she'd parked a few
blocks from the scene.

As Mike had griped, everyone else had
beaten her there. Because she'd lingered

behind at the estate, talking to a confused child. The kid had to just be confused; she probably had no idea what her father had been going through as the empire he'd spent his life building crumbled around him. Angry and frustrated, he must have seemed like a completely different man to his daughter.

Hell, even to Jillian who hardly knew him, he'd seemed like a completely different man. He definitely hadn't been the man who'd fascinated and attracted her the past few years. But then she'd been more attracted to the myth than the reality. Was he the reality or someone else? An imposter?

"You're losing it, Jill," she scoffed at herself. She was getting almost as paranoid as those people who proclaimed the end was near. She saw monsters everywhere now...because she'd missed seeing them when she should have.

She clicked the remote keyless entry on her car and pulled open her door. As she slid behind the wheel, she sniffed the air. Even inside, it was thick with smoke from the building blocks away. But mingled with the smoke was the faint odor of leather...and blood. Her heart slammed against her ribs as she realized she was not the only one in her car. Her hand trembling, she reached for the door handle, but a black glove closed over her mouth. And a steely arm locked around her shoulders, holding her against the seat.

She thrashed, fighting against his grasp. Lifting her keys, she swung them backward.

"You didn't fight me last night," he murmured in that raspy whisper. His glove slid away from her mouth, the leather gliding across her cheek, before he twisted the ring of keys from her grasp.

He was supposed to be dead; she'd seen for herself what she'd believed was his body being carried from the remains of the bombed-out building.

She shivered and gasped for breath. And ignored that traitorous flash of relief that he lived. But then, no matter what destruction he'd caused, she owed him. "Last night you saved my life."

Irony in his raspy voice, he asked, "So that I could take it tonight?"

She'd like to know why he had saved her, but something else was more important. "You're supposed to be dead."

"Yeah," he agreed. "But I'm not."

She glanced into the rearview mirror, but

all she glimpsed was her own pale face and the hulking shadow looming over her. "Who was in that body bag?"

"You don't need to know that," he replied, his voice never rising above that raspy whisper.

"I'll find out soon enough," she reminded him, "when the autopsy is complete."

"There won't be an autopsy," he said.

"Why not?"

"Because there is no body."

She tried to fight again, thrashing on the seat, but his grasp was too tight. She'd thought him crazy before for taking on Tobias St. John. Now she had her proof. Panting from her futile exertion, she said, "I saw them load the body into the van. We have footage of it."

"The body won't make it to the morgue."

She shivered again. "How can you know that…unless…?"

"I'm here," he pointed out. "With you. I won't be the one hijacking the hearse."

"Why are you here?" she asked. "Who are you? Why are you doing this?"

"So many questions, Miss Drake." He tsked with a rusty-sounding chuckle.

"Are you going to answer any of them?"
"No."

"Then I don't understand what you want with me." Except that maybe he regretted having spared her life the night before…

"I WANT YOU…" His throat closed—probably from the smoke he'd inhaled. Not with desire. Sure, Jillian Drake was beautiful, but she was also dangerous—with all her questions and all her ambition. That was why he had always stayed away from her. And why he shouldn't be around her now.

Except that he needed her.

"I want you to report a story."

In the rearview mirror, her green eyes widened with surprise and sparkled with excitement. "You're going to give me an exclusive?"

"I'm going to give you a statement."

"Let me call my crew. We'll do an on-camera interview." She reached into her purse and pulled out her phone, but he grabbed it from her.

"You don't need this," he assured her as he tossed the phone onto the floor. His grip loosened; she squirmed around on the seat, her breasts pushing against his arm.

"Let me go!" she demanded.

As beautiful as she was, she was undoubtedly used to men rushing to do her bidding. He did no one's bidding but his own. He tightened his grip again, grunting as his bruised ribs pushed against the seat between them.

"You're hurt?" she asked, her body stilling. "Were you wounded in the explosion?"

"Enough with the questions," he snapped. He couldn't waste any more time with her, not with what was at stake. St. John might think he had no reason to hold on to his leverage any longer. *He* had to prove the man wrong. Again.

"Please, tell me what's going on," she urged him. "You can trust me."

He'd learned long ago to never trust a woman, but he needed her. "There's only one thing you need to know, that you have to report as soon as possible."

"Your statement," she said. "What is it? What do you want me to tell the city?"

"I'm not dead."

Her lips parted on a short laugh. "That's it? That's my big exclusive?"

"It's something no one else knows," he pointed out. Something he could have shared with any other reporter, but he'd wanted her to be the one to break the news.

"You're right," she agreed. "Even before tonight, everyone called you a ghost, a phantom. After tonight, after footage of that body being loaded into the coroner's van, no one will believe you're alive."

"Then you'll have to convince them." Because he needed one man to believe that he was alive, but he couldn't risk telling St. John personally. Not yet.

And that was why he'd chosen her. It was the only reason he could have had. "People trust you."

"People," she said with a slight smile. "But not you."

He shook his head, and then realizing she couldn't see his action, he replied, "No."

"Why should I report your statement?" she asked. "What's in it for me?"

Damn. She had just proven why he shouldn't trust her. Rage coursed through him, and he tightened his arm around her. "*Your* life."

"What? Are you threatening me?" she asked, her voice cracking with anger rather than fear. But her green eyes widened with apprehension that belied her bravado. "If I don't say what you want, you're going to kill me? Like you killed those other women?"

"Do you really think I had something to do with those women dying?" If she did, he suspected she'd be fighting him harder than she had.

"I don't know," she admitted. "I'm not sure you were even around when those murders happened."

God, she was good. But he wasn't about to supply her with his alibi.

"Tell me if you hurt them," she said. "Tell me if you're going to hurt me…."

Until tonight he hadn't realized that people might die, that people might have to die, in order for him to achieve his goal. But could he actually *kill?*

"WHILE THE CORONER'S office confirms that the body from the explosion has disappeared, this reporter can personally assure you that the suspect that witnesses have described as the man with no face—among some other colorful nicknames—is still alive."

St. John hurled his glass at the flat screen.

Scotch streamed down the beautiful face of Jillian Drake. "You're lying!" he accused the image on TV.

"I don't think so," a soft voice murmured.

He whirled toward the woman who'd stepped inside the dark-paneled den. "She's a liar. She has to be."

Susan shook her head. "No. She told me earlier tonight—after you left her here—that she would never report anything she couldn't prove."

With a shaking fist, he gestured toward the screen. "She has no proof. Nothing but her word."

Susan's shoulders lifted in a slight shrug. "I don't think she'd give her word unless she knew for certain."

"You think she's seen him?" *Son of a bitch*—the man had to be dead. He *had* to be....

Susan nodded. "Yes."

"But I saw him—his body." An hour ago, before he'd had it destroyed. "He was the same build, with the same tattoo on his arm."

She shuddered and asked, "Did you see his face?"

"No." He'd had no face left. St. John had

laughed at the irony of that. But was the last laugh on him? "Damn him!"

"What about fingerprints or DNA?" she asked anxiously. "Can you test for that?"

"Not now." Not with the body completely burned up. He'd had to destroy it, so that no one else would be able to confirm the identity of the dead man. But now he had no confirmation, either.

He'd wanted—he needed—the man to be dead, but every instinct had screamed at him that he wasn't. His enemy had already proved he was not that easy to get rid of....

"So what do we do?" Susan asked.

"We beef up security." He'd already done that at the estate, and even as each business had been attacked, he hadn't spared any of the staff to guard them, which many people—including his security staff—had questioned. But he knew the plan was to distract him from what his enemy wanted most. St. John would *not* be distracted.

Susan turned to the windows and gestured toward the bars on them. "The place is already a fortress."

"It's not good enough!" he shouted at her. "If he's still out there, he'll be coming for..."

He swallowed hard. He wasn't certain what his enemy wanted. If it were him, he'd be after the money, the power and the vengeance. But he didn't know his enemy as well as he thought he had, as he should.

"If you think you know what he wants, why don't we just get rid of it?" she asked, her dark eyes wide with fear.

He laughed at her ignorance. But her stupidity was the only reason he'd kept her around. "If we got rid of what he wants, he'd have nothing to lose."

She shuddered again. "Oh, God…"

"And there's no one more dangerous than a man with nothing to lose." A lesson he had learned long ago. The one that had brought him to River City.

Susan must have been smart enough to sense the desperation he felt because she backed toward the door. "I better go up. I better check on the little girl—makes sure she's really sleeping now."

He waved her off, then clicked an intercom button. "I need to see you."

Within minutes the chief of the security team stood before him. Unlike everyone else, this man—Morris—was the only one who wasn't a new hire. St. John had gotten rid of the old team because he'd needed men he could trust. He still wasn't sure he could trust Morris so he hadn't let him too close and mostly assigned him to just guard the gates. But St. John needed him. No one knew the estate like Nick Morris.

"Did you see Jillian Drake's report on the eleven o'clock news?" he asked the blond man. "She claims the dead man wasn't the one who's been behind all the break-ins and explosions."

"You saw him."

St. John had made certain he'd been the only one, besides the coroner's assistants, who had seen the body. Those men had had no idea who they'd been looking at, especially as the man had had no face.

"So was it him?" Morris asked.

"I thought so." He'd hoped so. "But now she's reporting that he's still alive. Could she be lying?" He wanted Susan to be wrong; after all, she was new to River City and not the best judge of character. "Reporters lie, right?"

Morris shook his head. "Not Jillian Drake. She has a reputation for reporting facts. Not

rumors or myths like some of the other networks. Hell, she's never specifically reported
anything about him until tonight. He must
have talked to her. He must be alive."

"You know what this means," St. John said,
pouring himself another drink to replace the
one that had stained the plasma screen.

Morris sighed. "He's still out there."

"That." *Damn him to hell and back*. "And
he wasn't working alone."

Morris shrugged broad shoulders. "Guess
it would have been pretty hard for him to do
all that destruction by himself. He must have
had a partner."

"Yeah," St. John agreed, and he turned his
focus on the former chief of security, studying
the man.

"That guy's dead, though," Morris said.

"It would have been pretty hard for him
to pull off all those heists and explosions by
himself," St. John mused. "He gets around
the security systems. Cleans the place out and
then blows it up. That's a hell of a lot for one
or even two men to pull off." The man was
damn dangerous enough on his own, but with
help…

"So you think there're more of them out there?" Morris asked.

"Yeah," St. John replied. "I think he has more help."

"Who?"

He stared at Morris's face, his eyes narrowed as he continued to study him. "I don't know. You tell me who'd be stupid enough to take *me* on. It'd have to be someone close to him. Or someone close to me..."

Morris stared off in the distance. "The enemies of thy enemy are thy friends..."

"That's quite profound." Especially coming from the muscle-head St. John had always figured Morris to be. He had underestimated the guy; he never should have trusted him.

Morris chuckled. "Hey, just repeating what I've heard you say before."

St. John had only enemies. And it was well past time he got rid of them. *All.*

Chapter Five

"I've told you everything that happened," she insisted, her eyes gritty with fatigue. The police had picked her up immediately following her last broadcast.

"He just accosted you on the street at the crime scene? How come no one else saw him?" Sergeant Breuker persisted.

"Everyone else had left for the morgue." For no reason. Just as he'd predicted, the body had never arrived. "What are you doing to find the missing coroner's van?" Fortunately, the attendants had not been harmed, as they had conveniently left the vehicle unattended while it had been stolen. Obviously someone had paid them or threatened them into leaving it unlocked in the parking lot of the city morgue. It had to have been St. John. Because if the man she'd called Dante had had the body, he wouldn't have needed her to make the special report that had landed her in an interrogation room.

Color flushed the sergeant's face. "We have units looking for it."

"You have all your units looking for *him*." The man with no face…

"Is he really out there, Miss Drake, or have you just invented this story as a way to increase your station's ratings?"

She lifted her shoulders in a shrug. She could have proved her statement. After the man had left her car, she'd found blood smeared on the backseat. But if she shared that information with the police, they would confiscate her car. Though she doubted it would ever make it to the impound lot, just like the body had not made it to the morgue. Was there anyone not on St. John's payroll? Besides her?

"I don't care if you believe me," she said, "just let me go. You can't keep me here unless you're going to charge me with something."

"Obstructing justice, Miss Drake, comes to mind," the sergeant threatened for the umpteenth time.

"Freedom of the press," Jillian shot back

at him for the umpteenth time. "I have every right to protect my sources."

A knock at the door drew the sergeant's attention from her. The door of the small windowless interrogation room opened, and broad shoulders filled the doorway as Tobias St. John stepped inside. "I have some questions for the reporter, Sergeant."

"You called him?" Jillian asked Breuker. "You told him you picked me up." Hell, St. John had probably ordered them to pick her up.

"The police department has been gracious enough to keep me apprised of their investigation," he answered for the officer. "Thank you, Sergeant," he said, dismissing the older man.

The police officer hesitated for just a moment before stepping outside and closing the door behind him, locking Jillian in alone with Tobias St. John. To keep anyone from interrupting their conversation or to keep Jillian from escaping? She resisted the urge to run for the door and hammer at it. They had no right to lock her up, no right to keep her at all unless they pressed charges. But curiosity overrode her concern for her personal safety.

Tobias St. John stepped closer to the table, slammed his palms on the metal surface and leaned across it until his face nearly touched hers. "Why won't you extend me that same courtesy, Miss Drake?"

"What?" She pushed back her chair, easing away from his angry face. She was curious, not stupid.

"Why won't you keep me apprised of your investigation?"

"I'm not like River City's finest," she said. "I don't answer to you."

He laughed. "That's about to change, Miss Drake. I just put in an offer for WXXM. Soon I'll be your boss."

As he already was everyone else's, except the man with no face. She would have thought Dante answered to no one, until his admission the night before.

"What is it, Miss Drake?" St. John asked. His blue eyes narrowed as he studied her face. "For once, you're speechless."

She sighed. "No. It's just that I wish I had nothing to say." But St. John had a right to know what she'd learned.

"But you do know something," he surmised, "something you haven't admitted to the ineffective Sergeant Breuker?"

"I'm good at my job," she said. And because she was, she hadn't let Dante leave her car without answering at least one question for her.

As his arm had slid from around her shoulders, she'd clutched at it, holding it close to her chest so he could feel the pounding of her heart. "I won't report your statement," she'd boldly threatened him. "And killing me won't get the word out that you're alive."

"I'm not going to kill you," he'd assured her.

She'd expelled a shaky breath of relief then, even though she would have been foolish to trust him to keep his word. Hell, she'd be foolish to trust anyone at all

"But I can't believe you're willing to give up an exclusive," he'd mused, his raspy voice full of doubt.

"Exclusive?" She'd snorted. "You're not dead. Some breaking news," she'd scoffed. "Who the hell are you?"

He'd leaned over the back of the seat, his

mouth so close to her ear that his lips brushed the lobe. "I'm not telling you that."

She'd glanced into the rearview mirror, but all she'd seen was the top of his head, the thick dark hair that fell over his face. "I call you Dante," she'd admitted.

He'd laughed that gruff, rusty-sounding chuckle. "That actually fits more than…"

"Your real name?"

"I'm not answering that."

"Just one," she'd negotiated. "Answer one question honestly and I'll make the statement for you."

While he'd continued to hold on to her with his right arm, the gloved hand of his left one moved over her face and down her neck. His fingers wrapped around her throat. "You think you're in any position to be making deals with me?"

"You just admitted that you're not going to kill me," she'd said, forcing certainty into her voice, even though she'd felt none. She'd been lied to before, many times.

"What do you want to know?"

"I think you know."

"I'm not revealing my identity." His grip had eased on her throat, his fingers stroking her skin as if to soothe any hurt he might have inflicted.

Goose bumps had lifted along her arms, and she'd shivered.

"Hurry it up," he'd urged her. "You need to get out of here. File your report."

"*Your* report," she'd corrected him, her fingers still clutching the sleeve of his thick wool trench coat. "Which I won't make until I get one answer."

He'd laughed—another rusty-sounding chuckle. "You better make it a damn good question. And I told you, I'm not saying who I am," he said, his voice rough with impatience. "Your time's running out."

Panic had rushed over her. And she, who had never been at a loss for questions, floundered for one that he might actually deign to answer. Then she'd remembered St. John's suspicions. "Are you working for someone else?"

"What do you mean?"

"Are you doing all of this—breaking into and blowing up St. John's businesses—for someone else?"

"Yes," he'd replied without hesitation, his voice deep with an urgency she didn't understand. But then she really didn't understand anything about his war against Tobias St. John.

Disappointment had flashed through her, easing her grip on his arm. And he'd pulled free. But before he'd opened the door of the backseat, he'd leaned over her again. She'd felt the skim of his lips, and the heat of his breath against her cheek—and then she'd felt the supple caress of leather. But his hands weren't on her.

And when she'd glanced in the rearview mirror this time, she'd seen his face—or she would have, had he not been wearing a leather mask.

The man with no face…

Fingers snapped in front of her, bringing Jillian back to the present and St. John's face, his chiseled cheekbones flushed with anger and impatience. "You have something to say to me…you damn well *say* it!"

"I, uh…" She blinked, pushing thoughts of the man in the mask from her mind. "You were right."

St. John eased back again, his eyes still narrowed with the suspicion that seemed such a part of his personality. Mistrust was a trait that Jillian could relate to. "What about?"

"He *is* working for someone else," she explained. "He admitted it to me."

"Did he tell you who?"

She shook her head. "He wouldn't say." He hadn't said anything else, and she'd been too stunned over seeing the mask to ask him anything before he'd slipped away, leaving behind only those thick smears of blood on the light gray leather of her backseat. And on her fingertips from where she'd touched him. He was mortal all right, maybe even mortally wounded.

St. John laughed and shook his head as if he pitied her. "I guess now we know why he kept you alive the other night."

"We do?"

"He's using you," he said with a grin, "to send messages to me."

She shrugged, unable to deny that she'd let herself be used. But this time, at least, she'd been aware. And she'd gotten something out of it—that exclusive he'd promised.

"I'd be careful, Miss Drake," he warned, leaning across the table again. He touched her face, sliding a rough fingertip along her jaw. "Even a woman as beautiful as you are can outlive her usefulness. The next time he grabs you, he probably won't let you live."

"He's not a killer," she said.

"Someone died last night," he reminded her, "in an explosion *he* caused. That makes him a killer."

Her mystery man hadn't offered any explanation for the other man's death, hadn't sworn it an accident. He'd done nothing but leave that blood behind in her car. His? Or his victim's?

"Who was it that died last night?" she asked.

St. John lifted those broad shoulders in a shrug. "I don't know."

"I guess we'll never know since his body disappeared," she said, studying his icy blue eyes for a flicker of guilt.

But he betrayed no emotion. Was he capable of feeling anything besides anger? "Your friend didn't tell you last night?" he taunted her. "Because I'm sure you asked."

"No, he didn't," she admitted. "I don't know if the dead man was working with him or helping you. Did you have guards stationed at the jewelry store?"

St. John shook his head, but not in response to her question as he said, "You're the one under interrogation, Miss Drake. Not me."

"I've told the police everything I know," she insisted, her head pounding with frustration that she didn't know more. Sure, she'd convinced him to answer one question, but it wasn't the question she'd really wanted answered.

As if he'd read her mind, St. John cautioned her. "Be careful what you learn, Miss Drake. It may be enough to get you killed."

"Are you threatening me?" she asked, with a glance to the door. Not that it would matter if the police sergeant had overheard it; he wouldn't do anything to St. John, not with all the commerce and humanitarian awards the mayor had heaped upon him over the years. Until recently, she'd believed he'd deserved them; she'd nearly believed the good press all his generous donations had bought him.

"I'm offering you some friendly advice," St. John replied, but there was nothing remotely friendly about the cold gleam in his ice-blue eyes. "You've let a dangerous man use you. If you get too close to him, you're only going to wind up hurt. Or worse."

Was St. John right? If she ran into the masked man again, would she become his next victim?

"DEATH WAS ALWAYS a possibility," the man in the leather mask said. "I warned you all up front that this was a dangerous mission." But still the tight knot of guilt in his gut didn't ease. It didn't matter that they had been aware of the risks; it hadn't felt real until now.

"You giving us an out?" someone asked from the shadows. These men—men who'd committed themselves to helping him take down St. John—had been living in the shadows with him. In his own personal hell. Jillian Drake's nickname for him fit far more than she knew.

"No. That was another warning I gave you up front," Dante reminded them. "Once you're in, there's only *one* way out." The way his friend had gone the night before.

Fear flickered in their eyes and added tension to the already thick atmosphere of the dark tunnel. Despite the faint light, Dante could see their faces and their regrets. They wondered now if they'd backed the right man, or if he was more dangerous than the man they were going after. He could have answered their unspoken question, but the truth would only add to their fear and regret.

"We're close," he assured them. "It'll be over soon." Hopefully with the outcome he'd planned. Or else he might as well die, too.

"What about the reporter—Jillian Drake?" asked one of the soldiers in the war he'd declared.

"What about her?" Dante asked, his lips twitching as he remembered the sweetness of her skin against them.

"She's trouble."

He'd figured that out for himself a long time ago. And now, having touched her silky skin, having felt the curve of her breasts, the heat of her breath…she'd become a distraction he couldn't afford.

That same nervous soldier warned him, "She could blow everything up."

And that was *his* job. To destroy everything St. John had claimed for himself until the man had nothing left and nowhere to go but the hell to which he'd sent Dante.

"I won't allow her to interfere," he assured his crew. Sticking to the plan he'd made was the only thing keeping him going, keeping him sane—especially now that he'd lost one of his friends.

"You think she's going to let up until she uncovers the whole truth?" one of the men asked.

"No," he admitted. She was too ambitious. Yet this was about more than ambition or greed; at least, to him it was. And that was why he couldn't let Jillian interfere. If she found out about his plan before he'd had a chance to carry it out, she could cost him what mattered most to him. "But I'll stop her before she figures it out."

"How?"

"By whatever means necessary…"

THE DOOR TO Franklin Eberhardt's house stood ajar. Jillian's fingers trembled as she reached out for it.

"Hello?" she called out. "Hello? Is anyone home?"

Where was the man's security system? His bodyguards? St. John had all that and more. But then he needed them. St. John was the one under attack. She should have been with Charlie and Vicky, staking out one of the billionaire's remaining businesses. She should have been waiting for the next bombing.

But she didn't want to wait for something to happen; she wanted to find out why it was happening in the first place. And so she had to find someone who would actually answer the questions everyone else kept ignoring.

She wasn't too hopeful, though, that Eberhardt would consent to an interview. None of the other people on the list she'd compiled of St. John's enemies had been willing to talk to her. She suspected, though, that fear more than guilt had kept them silent.

Not that Franklin Eberhardt had any real reason to seek vengeance. Sure, St. John had bought out his furniture factory, but Eberhardt would have lost it had the former marine turned entrepreneur not convinced him to sell it to him before the foreclosure.

"Mr. Eberhardt?" Her voice echoed in the eerie silence.

She pushed the door just far enough open that she could step inside. While the house wasn't as opulent as St. John's estate, the contemporary structure had soaring ceilings and walls of glass. Burnished sunshine, the last rays of the setting sun, bathed the off-white carpet.

This wasn't a frightening place; there were no shadows or raspy whispers. Still, goose bumps lifted along Jillian's arms, and the nape of her neck tingled. Her instincts alerted her that she'd stumbled into a dangerous situation.

"Mr. Eberhardt?" she called out as she stepped into the bright living room. She'd never backed down from danger before, especially not when she was on the verge of cracking a story.

A noise drew her attention to the windows just as one pane shattered. She flinched and screamed. "Mr. Eberhardt?"

Another pane shattered, bits of glass flying like a hard rain off concrete. Another scream tore free of her throat as pain pierced her shoulder. Blood—warm and sticky—trickled down her arm. Was it glass or…a bullet that had grazed her skin?

Her heart pounding at a frantic rate, she dropped to her stomach. Shots, probably fired from a gun with a silencer, continued to shatter the windows in the living room. Shards of glass rained down onto her back and into her hair.

Those shards of broken glass sparkled in the rays of dying sunshine, the light bouncing back at her. She had to find a way out of here. But if she walked outside, she would have no protection. Her cheek pressing deep into the soft carpet, she turned her head and stared into the open, dead eyes of Franklin Eberhardt.

Like her, he lay on his side on the carpet but on the other side of the couch. The tall legs of the sofa held it high enough off the ground that she could see all of the dead man as well as the blood pooled around him. A bullet hole had broken the skin between those sightless eyes.

Someone out there was determined to do the same thing to her.

And she had no idea how to save herself.

Chapter Six

"You didn't miss anything," Vicky's assuring voice came over her cell phone. "Nothing happened tonight."

No one, including her, had reported what had happened at Eberhardt's house. The police hadn't been thrilled by her not so veiled innuendoes that they were working for St. John, and they would probably arrest her for Eberhardt's murder, instead of protecting her.

Did she need protection? Had someone really been trying to kill her?

She couldn't stop her teeth from chattering, couldn't stop shaking in reaction. She'd lain there a long time, staring into the eyes of the dead man, until she'd thought it safe—and dark enough—to come out of the house. And when she'd finally risen to her shaking legs, she'd crouched low, and prayed and run for her car. But even now, blocks from the murder scene, she couldn't catch her breath. She couldn't slow her heart rate from its fast and furious pace.

"Jillian?" Vicky called through the cell phone. "You still there?"

"Yeah, yeah…" But she could barely believe it herself. Someone had been shooting at her. Had the shots been a murder attempt or just a warning?

"I thought the signal got lost for a minute there," the young producer commented.

"No, I'm here." But was she? As she drove, she peered through the windshield, looking for the right street. Although the man she'd hoped to interview had been dead, she hadn't left Eberhardt's house empty-handed. As she'd lain there, across from his body, she'd noticed the scrap of paper clasped tight in his fingers. And she'd eased under the couch and pried the paper from his cold, dead hand.

She glanced down at it now. The glow from the dash illuminated the few letters and numbers left on the torn scrap of what might have been a property deed. This industrial section of River City was filled with factories and warehouses; every other one burned out and boarded up. Maybe those picketers with the end-is-near signs were right. At least, they nearly had been in her case.

"Jillian? Are you okay?"

No. She was as crazy as those picketers for following up the dead man's lead all by herself. Tears stung her eyes, but she couldn't share her fears with her young friend. She couldn't put Vicky and Charlie in danger, too. And she damn well couldn't trust the police. That was why she'd had to come alone. "Fine. I'm fine…"

"Can I ask you something, then?"

"Yeah…" But she probably wouldn't reply; she much preferred asking the questions to answering them.

"Did you really see him last night?"

"What?"

"The man with no face? Was it really him? Is he really still alive?"

Maybe the girl had a future in front of the camera, asking the hard questions. "Why would you ask that?"

"It's not that I don't believe you," Vicky hastily assured her. "It's just that nothing happened tonight. And for the past two weeks something has every night—sometimes twice a night. It's just weird."

But something had happened. Instead of blowing up buildings, he'd started shooting people? She couldn't believe that—or she didn't want to—until she had proof of his guilt.

"Are you sure he was real? What you saw last night?" Vicky persisted. "Maybe he was just a ghost."

"Everybody's been calling him a ghost— a phantom—these weeks, and that hasn't stopped him from attacking St. John's businesses," she reminded her friend.

But he'd only ever attacked St. John. So why would he have switched to Eberhardt? And forgone explosives for bullets? Except for the torn deed, she hadn't noticed anything missing. While the picture concealing the safe behind the couch had been removed, the safe door had been closed and locked.

"Vicky, I need to tell you something," she said, because she needed another opinion, someone to help her figure out what the hell was going on, to continue the investigation in case something happened to her.

"Jill—" Vicky's voice broke off to a rush of static in the cell.

Hell! She glanced down at the phone's LCD screen, which displayed a no-signal message. She had lost it now, along with any hope of getting help if her little lead led her into danger again.

She fought back the panic that had her breathing faster. All she had to do was turn around and drive back to the spot where she'd had a connection. Then she would stop being foolhardy and call for help. Steadied with resolve, she pressed on the accelerator and headed toward an alley where she could turn around. But before she'd passed many of those abandoned-looking warehouses, a loud crack startled her into cringing and ducking.

God, had the shooter followed her? She'd been careful to watch the rearview mirror and hadn't noticed any cars behind her. No other cars were on the road at all, not this late past curfew.

The steering wheel jerked to the left. Then rubber slapped against asphalt. The tire had blown. Her breath shuddered out in a relieved sigh. But then she tightened her hands around the wheel, fighting to keep the car from jumping onto the curb. The headlights glinted on the blackened walls of a burned-out metal warehouse, and yellow crime-scene tape fluttered free from a lamppost.

She'd been a fool for coming here alone, and she'd played the fool too many times already. But this time was worse; tonight it had been her choice.

"This is crazy," she murmured.

Having had her fill of crime scenes for the night, she pressed down on the accelerator, ignoring the flat. The wheel shuddered beneath her hands as the car fought her efforts. Yet she stopped only when the bare rim ground against the road, sparks igniting off the metal striking the asphalt.

Streetlamps were broken out and glass littered around the bases of the iron poles. She had no light but for the dim glow from the dash. She checked the door locks, then reached for her phone again. But the cell still got no reception. Tears of frustration stung her eyes. "What the hell am I going to do...?"

Impatient with her momentary weakness, she blinked back the moisture. Growing up the way she had, she'd learned young how to protect herself, or she wouldn't have survived.

She could damn well change her own tire. She reached for the trunk button on the car's keyless remote and clicked it. Then, her hand trembling slightly, she unlocked her door and stepped onto the dark, deserted street.

She'd proved long ago—as well as just hours before—that she was a survivor.

Armageddon wasn't coming for her....

"FIND THAT LITTLE BITCH and bring her to me!" St. John demanded, slamming his fist onto the desk in the den.

Morris gestured for other guards to carry out the order while he remained behind, standing near the open door. "We'll find her."

"She lied," St. John said, fury boiling inside him. "She must have lied...."

"So you think he's dead now?"

"Nothing happened tonight. He must be dead." But that niggling doubt remained, twisting his guts into knots, pounding with the tension at his temples.

Morris nodded. "Sure..."

The doubt was in the security chief's voice.

"What do you think?" St. John asked now,

caring for the first time about the other man's opinion.

Morris shrugged. "He could be dead...or he could be planning something big."

And St. John had just sent off the majority of his guards to find Jillian Drake. Had she become a distraction?

BEFORE LEANING into her open trunk, Jillian nervously glanced around the deserted street. If someone shot at her now, using that gun with a silencer, she would never notice the bullets coming until it was too late. She shook her head, thoroughly disgusted with herself. She'd been crazy to come out alone to an address she'd found in a dead man's hand.

But then her judgment hadn't always been the best. Case in point: her cheating ex-husband. With a sigh, she heaved the spare tire from her trunk and fumbled for the jack beneath it. She dropped it onto the street next to the spare, then grabbed the tire iron—just as someone grabbed her.

Big arms wrapped tight around her, pinning her arms to her sides. She kicked out, but he lifted her feet above the ground. Her heels connected with shins as hard as cement columns. The man holding her didn't even grunt, just as he hadn't when he'd carried her to safety two nights ago. It had to be Dante. He was so big, so strong, and still that faint odor of smoke clung to him along with another musky scent that was his alone.

She didn't trust that he intended to carry her to safety this time. Even without St. John's warning ringing in her ears, she would have been afraid of him. Because he'd found her here, where a dead man had led her.

He'd rescued her that first night they'd met, so she'd painted him in the same romantic light some of the witnesses had. But he wasn't some well-intentioned robber, stealing from the rich to give to the poor. Nor was he some misunderstood, gentle monster.

Eberhardt's face flashed through her mind. After staring at it for hours, she wasn't likely to ever forget the look in those dead eyes. The surprise and the fear.

This man really was a monster; he was a killer.

She kicked harder and screamed, straining her throat with her efforts to attract attention. But not a single shadow stirred but him. "Let me go!"

"Shh," he advised her in that familiar, raspy whisper. "You have to get out of here!"

"So let me go!" She drew up her knee, so she could kick him where it would count. But he shifted his stance and caught her leg between his thighs. She wriggled, loosening his arms enough that she was able to swing the tire iron in her hand and connect with his ribs.

This time he grunted, his breath stirring her hair. But instead of letting her go, he tightened his hold and moved toward the center of the street.

She hadn't noticed any cars following hers. She had seen no other vehicle on the road at all. Where was he taking her? Into one of the buildings? They were all deserted at this hour of night. Metal clanged as he kicked aside a manhole cover. Then, with her still clasped tight against him, he stepped inside the hole.

Jillian closed her eyes and tensed, expecting a fall, waiting for their bodies to hit either sewage or cement. But his boots struck each rung of the ladder leading down into the underground tunnels. He removed one arm from around her so that his gloved hand could hold the side of the ladder, guiding them down into the torch-lit tunnel.

If he only wanted to talk to her, as he had those other times before, he would have left her on the street. He wouldn't drag her down into the sewer.

Jillian took advantage of his loosened hold to fight again. She kicked, but she didn't have her heels as weapons now. They'd dropped either onto the street or into the sewer. Her ankle struck the steel ladder. Pain radiated up her leg and down to her toes, the intensity of it bringing tears to her eyes. But she blinked away the stinging moisture and swung the tire iron again, hoping this time to connect with his head. Instead, she struck his shoulder, which was strong and broad.

No wonder so many witnesses had described him as a monster; he was so big. Tall and muscular. His boots kicked up water as he jumped from the last rung onto the tunnel floor. Jillian, desperate to escape before he took her any deeper underground, wriggled and kicked, fighting with all the strength she had.

His hold finally loosened enough that she broke free, falling onto her knees in the water.

Before he could reach for her again, she spun around, with the tire iron raised to defend herself.

Her breath left her lungs in a rush. He was even bigger than she had remembered. His shoulders were impossibly broad, making her wonder how he'd managed to get them through the manhole opening. His chest was muscular, so much that his black wool trench coat didn't close over it. The torches in the tunnel illuminated the mask she'd only glimpsed in the dark the night before. The supple black leather molded to his face as if a part of it. Except for holes through which his dark eyes glittered, the leather covered from his forehead to the curve of his upper lip.

Her fingers trembled around the tire iron she clenched. If he really was what all those witnesses claimed—inhuman—how could she hope to defend herself with just a metal rod?

"I did what you asked of me," Jillian reminded him. "I reported that you're still alive. What do you want with me now?"

"Nothing."

She swallowed the gasp of surprise and fear. St. John had been right. Now that she was no longer of use to this man, he intended to get rid of her. She tightened her grasp on her weapon. Unlike Franklin Eberhardt who'd looked so surprised, she wouldn't go down without a fight.

JILLIAN DRAKE, her famous face smeared with grease from the tire iron she held, stood ankle deep in the sewer water. She had made a career of going anywhere for a story, but even she would not have voluntarily come down here. To hell.

But she had left him no choice. He couldn't leave her up *there,* interfering with his plan. But down here—with him—she was still interfering. With his head.

She was so damned beautiful with her porcelain skin and long, wavy red hair. And those eyes, those heavily lashed green eyes that stared out of the television screen every night, stared at him now—wide with fear. While he'd grown used to people being afraid of him, her fear struck him like a hard slap to his face. If he still had a face...

But he had lost that along with his identity. And maybe his humanity. No matter how afraid she was, he could not let her go.

She backed toward the ladder to the street, but he followed her, matching her step for step. "Stay away from me!" she shrieked, waving the tire iron in the air between them. "Don't touch me!"

He waited until she was backed against the ladder, and reached for her again. Screaming, she swung the tire iron toward his head. He caught the heavy metal in his gloved hand and jerked her forward, into his arms.

The softness and warmth of her wriggling body touched him, thawing the ice that had encased him for so long. As his pulse leaped in reaction to her closeness, he felt, if not entirely human, at least like a *man* for the first time in a long while.

"Let me go!" she yelled as she wrestled him for the tire iron.

"I can't." Dante effortlessly pulled the metal tool from her grasp and dropped it onto the tunnel floor, splashing them both with dirty water. Only rain runoff from the streets above fell into these sewers, and with rainfall low for the season, the water was shallow.

She lifted her gaze to his face—what she could see of his face. Her mouth had fallen open, as if she was shocked that he had taken her weapon. Like him, she wasn't used to people taking things away from her. Like him, she would probably never stop fighting to get back what was hers.

Her freedom. But that was the one thing he could not give her. It would cost them both too much. He grimaced as she shifted in his arms, nudging against his ribs, which were bruised from the explosion the night before and from her connecting with the tire iron. Grunting with pain, he loosened his hold and she pulled away from him.

"Don't hurt me," she said, more command than plea. Even afraid, the woman refused to betray any weakness.

The sleeve of her blouse was torn, and blood oozed from a scratch on her shoulder. "You're already hurt."

She glanced at her wound. "Did you do this?"

Regret clenched the muscles in his stomach. Had he scraped her shoulder when he'd carried her through the manhole? But if he'd left her up on the street—that street—she would have been hurt worse.

Her voice cracked now with the fear she'd

only previously betrayed with the vulnerability in her eyes. "Why do you want me dead?"

It was almost the last thing he wanted. That was why he'd grabbed her. And he reached out, intending to grab her again.

But she jerked away from him…just as the world shuddered. The explosives he'd set went off above them, the blast so powerful that the tunnels shook, knocking loose pieces of concrete and showering them with dust and debris. He dove for her, trying to shield her, but it was too late.

A chunk of rock struck her, knocking her back. He caught her before she hit the ground and swung her up in his arms. But she didn't fight him as she had before. She lay lifelessly, her head lolling back and her lids closed over those vibrant eyes.

Had he failed? Instead of protecting her life, had he taken it?

Chapter Seven

"He's not my daddy…" The little girl's voice, tremulous with fear, echoed inside Jillian's head.

Those eerily beautiful pale eyes desperately pleaded with her, as the child mouthed the words, *Help me…*

But Jillian hadn't helped Tabitha St. John. She'd put the child's fears from her mind and focused instead on the girl's father and on the man who'd targeted his empire. What about Tabitha? Who would protect the child?

Jillian, herself, had once been like that little girl, silently pleading that someone—anyone—would see the pain she was in and come to her aid. But no one had helped her. Just as she had not helped Tabitha St. John. Guilt pounded at her now, reverberating inside her skull.

Help me...

A scream tearing from her throat, Jillian jerked awake. Blinking in confusion, she glanced at her surroundings once her eyes adjusted to the faint glow from a wall sconce. She lay on a brass bed in some strange, windowless, concrete room. Fresh air pumped through vents in the ceiling so Jillian could breathe. But her lungs strained with the effort, panic pressing on them.

"Bad dream?" a raspy voice asked, and a shadow separated from the walls of the dimly lit room. He'd stood in front of a steel door, blocking it with his body. Blocking her escape even as he'd watched her sleep?

She shivered and agreed. "Nightmare."

He stepped farther away from the door. His thigh muscles stretched the seams of the black jeans he wore and his chest the cotton of his dark T-shirt beneath that open jacket. He moved closer to the bed; his dark gaze rested intently on her face before slipping down her body. During their struggle, a couple of buttons on her blouse had come undone, revealing the lace of her black bra. And her skirt had ridden up. He reached out with those big, gloved hands, and she shrank back against the metal headboard. But he didn't touch her; he only lifted a fleece blanket over her.

"I can understand why you're afraid," he said, but a muscle twitched along his tautly clenched jaw.

"I'm not afraid for me," she said. Not now. Not since she'd dreamed of Tabitha St. John and had felt her fear. If something happened to Jillian, though, who would come to the aid of the helpless child? Because Jillian had no doubt that the little girl had a reason for her fear. Tobias St. John was not the man everyone had always believed he was. She'd experienced his rage and ruthlessness herself. While he hadn't touched her, she didn't doubt he was capable of violence; it had been there in his eyes, barely restrained. God help whoever snapped that tenuous control….

"You should be afraid for you," the man said as he settled onto the bed next to her. He touched her now, sliding his gloved fingers into her hair. "How do you feel? Dizzy? Nauseated?"

"No." She winced as Dante probed a bump on the back of her head. "That hurts."

"You lost consciousness," he said, his voice

even raspier, as if her blacking out had affected him. "You probably have a concussion."

"I'm fine," she insisted. She'd had concussions before. If she had one now, it was slight. "What happened?" She remembered the earth shaking beneath her feet...and above her. "Another explosion?"

He nodded. "You're lucky you weren't killed."

"Isn't that what you want?" she asked, staring up at him in confusion. If only she could see his face...then she might be able to figure out if she had reason to fear him and to fight him.

"If I wanted you dead, do you really think you'd be here?" he replied. "In my *bed?*"

Was that why he'd kept her alive—because he wanted what so many other men had wanted from her? Just her body? Not her mind. Not her heart...

Rejecting her own foolishness, she shook her head and knocked his hand away. She didn't care what he wanted from her; he wasn't going to get it. Her heart pounded hard as anger coursed through her. "Then why shoot at me? Why nearly blow me up?"

"I didn't shoot at you."

"Yes, you did. It had to be you at Franklin Eberhardt's house." But she hoped it wasn't.

"No." His gloved hand touched her again, this time skimming over the cut on her shoulder. "Is that what caused this? A bullet?"

Biting her lip to hold in the cry she'd been too afraid to utter then, she nodded.

"It wasn't me," he insisted. "I don't even own a gun." And he lifted his arms, as if inviting her to frisk him.

"You do," she replied. "You must. You shot him."

"Who?"

"Franklin Eberhardt. He's dead."

A curse slipped through his lips, so involuntarily that there was no mistaking his genuine surprise. He shook his head, tumbling a lock of dark hair across his forehead, over the top of that leather mask. "No…"

"Was that the man—the one you're working for?"

He shook his head. "No."

"You have to be involved," she insisted. "He's the one who sent me here, to the warehouses you blew up tonight."

"You just said he was dead," he reminded her. "So how did he send you anywhere?"

"He had a piece of paper in his hand— part of a deed—with an address that brought me down here." Actually *he*—this mysterious masked man—had brought her down here in the tunnels, to safety. He'd rescued her again. Could he really be the killer Tobias St. John had claimed he was? That she had feared he was when she'd fought him?

He cursed again, his voice rough with emotion. "He used to own those warehouses, the ones that just blew up, before he sold them."

"To St. John," she said. "Do you think he shot Eberhardt?"

He shrugged, the impossibly broad shoulders rippling beneath the thin cotton of his T-shirt. "Why would he have…?"

She bit her lip again, as she realized what she'd done. "I think it's my fault. I think I killed that man."

CONNECTING WITH HER in a way he hadn't connected with anyone since he'd begun this new life—this miserable existence—he felt her pain, her guilt and regret. And so he closed his arms around her, pulling her tight against his chest. "You have nothing to do with any of this."

She shook her head, her hair brushing against his chin. "I told him. I told Tobias St. John what you said—about working for someone. Hell, I gave him a list of his enemies—as if he didn't already know who they were. But looking at it again, he must have believed it was Eberhardt who hired you."

"No." His arms tightened around her. "St. John already knows why I'm doing this and for whom."

She pulled back and stared up at him, her green eyes so full of questions. She only asked one of them. "Why?"

"Why would he kill Eberhardt?" He deliberately misunderstood. "Money. He has to be running out."

"How? He's a billionaire."

"He's also arrogant—too arrogant to think he needed insurance. He thought he'd be able to cover a loss if he had one."

"One," she said. "He's had more than one. Thanks to you almost everything's gone."

"So he has to be running out of money," Dante repeated. He had to be because it was part of the plan. "Since Eberhardt had part of a deed in his hand, St. John had probably offered him his company back." For a price.

And when Franklin hadn't been able or willing to pay it...

St. John was getting desperate since he was watching everything he'd wanted slip away from him. Soon it would be time for the final move in their game.

"Why are you doing this?" she asked. "Why are you going after Tobias St. John?"

"I can't tell you."

"You won't," she correctly surmised. "Is it all about money for you, too? Is that all you're after?"

He touched her face now, skimming the tip of his glove across her lips. "No more questions."

Her eyes filled with anger that glittered in the gold glints in the green. "Can't you see that the money isn't worth it? People are getting hurt. Killed."

Regret flashed through him, as his own guilt gnawed at him. He trailed his fingers down her throat to where her torn blouse revealed her wounded shoulder. As if he could kiss it better, he lowered his lips to the deep scratch.

She shivered.

"I'm sorry," he said. He'd never intended for

anyone to get hurt. And with the mask on, he couldn't offer her comfort—only more fear and unease. But hell, if he took it off, she'd be even more afraid and confused….

"I wasn't talking about myself," she said.

She never talked about herself, he realized now. She hadn't even been afraid for herself. "Who are you afraid for?" he wondered.

"An innocent child," she replied, her voice cracking with emotion. "She's caught up in the middle of this war you're waging against her father. And she's terrified."

He sucked in a breath as pain jolted him. "You talked to her?"

Jillian nodded. "I saw her. At his house. She asked me for help."

His heart clenched with regret. Soon. Soon he would be able to end the war…once he was certain that he would be victorious in the outcome. "None of this concerns you," he pointed out. "You need to stay out of it."

"I can't. I *need* to help her."

"Help her or help yourself to an exclusive?" he asked, doubtful that he'd been wrong about her. But just what kind of woman was Jillian Drake? Was there more to the ambitious reporter than he'd realized?

She sucked in an audible breath—of outrage. "I would never use a child."

"Then stay out of what you don't understand," he advised her.

She shook her head. "She asked me for help. I can't *not* help her."

"If you really want to help her, you need to get out of River City," he said. "You need to just *leave*."

Her green eyes widened with surprise. "You're going to let me go?"

"I'm not sure that I should," he admitted, his arms tightening around her, pulling her closer. She felt so good, her breasts crushed against his chest, her hair brushing against his chin and throat. He wasn't sure that he could let her go.

Her hands skimmed over his shoulders and trailed down his arms. "You can't keep me. That would be kidnapping."

"A little while ago you thought I was a killer," he reminded her. "You think that I would hesitate to kidnap someone? That I would worry about the consequences?" There was only one thing he worried about now.

"You have no reason to keep me," she insisted.

"For your safety." And his own peace of mind. "You said someone was shooting at you tonight. You're in danger."

She shook her head. "It wasn't personal. Nobody was trying to kill *me* specifically."

He couldn't imagine why anyone would be trying to kill Jillian. Besides him. It was his secret—his plan—that her prying threatened to expose.

"Are you sure about that?" he asked, wishing he could be as certain as she was that she wasn't really in danger.

"Yes," she insisted. "I was just in the wrong place at the wrong time. Like now."

Was she talking about his arms, or his bed or the underground room where he'd been forced to set up headquarters? All of them were the wrong place for her to be; he knew that, but he didn't loosen his hold on her.

She stared up at him, more questions swirling in those green eyes. "When I asked you earlier what you wanted with me, you said nothing," she reminded him of the words he'd spoken when he'd grabbed her out of the line of fire.

"Maybe I lied." To himself more than to her. He wanted Jillian Drake. Even though he'd known better than to trust her, he'd wanted Jillian for a long time.

She tensed in his arms and slid her palms between them, pushing against his chest. "You can't keep me here. People will miss me. They'll start looking for me."

"They won't find you here," he warned her. No one would think to look for Jillian Drake in the sewer.

She shivered again, and panic flashed in her eyes. But instead of pushing away from him, her hands stroked over his chest, and she batted her lashes at him. Her voice all breathy and sexy, she implored, "Please, let me go."

Even knowing she was using her feminine wiles to manipulate him, his pulse quickened. He had to let her go now, while he still could. His mouth curving into a grin, he complied. "Okay."

But when she moved to slide off the bed, he held on to her. "The only way you're leaving here, though, is with me." He had to make sure that she was really all right. When she'd lost consciousness, he'd barely found a pulse, had barely felt her breath against his skin when he'd lowered his face to hers. She seemed fine now, her pupils normal size, her face flushed instead of pale. She might be okay, but he had to ensure that she was safe.

She narrowed her eyes and studied his face, his mask. "But it must be almost dawn. You've never been seen out during the day."

"I've never been seen," he agreed. Because it would have broken the rules of the game even more than his late-night activities.

"You don't need that mask, do you?" she asked. "You're not hiding some disfigurement."

"How do you know?" he asked. Knowing what he did now, he wasn't certain he'd ever be able to remove the mask and look at his face again….

"I can see enough of it…" She lifted her fingertips and slid them along his jaw and over his lips.

He caught her wrist in his gloved hand, holding tight to her—not because he was worried that she might try to remove the mask, but because she made him want to remove it. She made him want…her.…

Her throat rippled as she swallowed. "You're not disfigured," she insisted. "You're hiding your identity."

"It doesn't matter who I am. I'm not a story

for you to break," he said. "Lives are at stake. Yours might be one of them." And that was partially his fault for involving her.

"I don't need you to protect me," she said.

"But you need me to get out of here." He let go of her for just a moment so he could take a silk scarf from his pocket and wrap it around her eyes. When she reached for the blindfold, he caught her wrists and bound those together.

She struggled with the bindings. "I thought you were letting me go."

"I am. I'm just not going to let you see where you've been." He couldn't trust that she wouldn't lead someone—either the police or St. John—right back to him. As she continued to fight against the scarves, he swung her up in his arms.

"How do I know you're really going to bring me out of here?" she asked, her voice trembling with nerves that betrayed the fear she'd earlier denied.

"You're going to have to trust me," he said.

"How can I trust you? I don't even know who—or *what*—you really are."

He chuckled. "You think I'm a phantom?" he asked. "Or a monster?"

"That's how witnesses have described you," she admitted.

"And yet you never reported that." Even though other networks, even other reporters at her same station, had. "You always knew I was a man." But, as if he needed to prove it, he lowered his mouth to hers.

LIPS STILL TINGLING from his kiss, Jillian leaned against the door of her apartment as if she'd just been dropped off after a date. But this was no date, despite the fact that he'd kissed her. And she'd kissed him back. When his lips had brushed her mouth and the mask her face, she'd gasped in surprise at the contact and the erotic pleasure that had jolted her pulse into overdrive.

He'd taken her parted lips as an invitation to deepen the kiss. His tongue sliding over hers, he'd made love to her mouth. The sensation— the heat and erotic flavor—had lightened her head and quickened her pulse. She wished she could have blamed her reaction on the blow she'd taken to her head. But the ache in her skull had receded to a dull throb.

She also wished she was the one who'd stopped the kiss. But he was the one who, with a groan, had pulled away from her. She couldn't even be sure that, if her hands had not been bound, she wouldn't have reached for him.

Her hands trembling, she tugged free the scarf he had loosened from around her wrists. It had definitely *not* been a date. And kissing him back had been as stupid as chasing down a dead man's lead.

She dragged off the blindfold he'd left on her the entire time he'd carried her home. He hadn't needed directions or an address; he'd known exactly where she lived. How? Because of her public profile, she was careful to keep her home address private.

But as she stared at the overturned furniture and ripped and torn clothing littering the hardwood floor, she realized she hadn't kept it private enough. Had he known where she lived because he'd done this?

She whirled back to the door, the one he'd told her to bolt behind him. Having thought the door locked and secured, he hadn't followed her inside. Because he hadn't wanted to see her reaction to this destruction?

She gasped at her mutilated belongings. She'd worked hard for those things, had fought hard for some of them in her divorce. But as she closed her eyes to shut out the sight, she saw again the face of the frightened child.

And she knew none of it mattered. She had to go back to St. John's, had to assure Tabitha that Jillian hadn't forgotten about her, that she wanted to help her. But as she headed into her bedroom to grab shoes and a change of clothes, a noise startled her.

Her heart pounding with fear, her body tense, she turned toward the fire escape just as a man stepped through the open window. Another man followed him; both of the burly men carried guns, which they pointed at her.

This close, they wouldn't miss. She swallowed hard, forcing down her fear. "What— what do you want?"

Had they been looking for something? What could they think she had?

"We've been waiting for you, Ms. Drake."

So they'd amused themselves by destroying her stuff? She bit her tongue to hold in the snarky question. "Why?"

"Mr. St. John wants to see you."

She nodded. "Good. I want to see him, too. Let me grab some clothes—"

One of the men grabbed her arm instead. "You don't look as pretty as you do on TV. Where have you been?"

"I don't know," she answered honestly. "Let me just clean up a minute."

The other man shook his head. "Mr. St. John won't mind. He's been waiting, too." A muscle twitched in his cheek as fear flickered in his eyes.

She doubted St. John had been any more patient than they had. "Then let's not keep him waiting any longer...." Even though she'd agreed to come without a fight, the first man swung her over his shoulder. They slammed out of her apartment and headed down the hall.

The sun had just begun to rise, light streaking across the sky and through the windows at the end of the hall. Her neighbors should have been rising for work, but no one opened their doors. Some creaked, though, as if some people leaned against them, peering through peepholes.

She opened her mouth to cry out for help. But who would her neighbors call? The police? They would deliver her to St. John just as quickly as his henchmen. Of course, his estate was where she'd intended to go, anyway. To talk to Tabitha.

But after what he'd ordered done to her apartment, she doubted he would let her speak to his daughter again. She suspected he didn't want Jillian talking to anyone anymore.

WHAT THE HELL ARE YOU DOING? With the sun rising, he had no time; he needed to be back underground before anyone saw him. He needed to be back with his crew, planning his next and hopefully last attack. He had no business standing here, in the shadow of Jillian Drake's apartment building.

But his gut clenched with foreboding. No birds chirped, and no dogs barked. Hell, he didn't even hear the engine of a car. It was too quiet. He'd had this feeling before—a lifetime ago when he'd been a marine in Special Forces. And two weeks ago, when he'd essentially lost his life.

He shouldn't have let her come back here. And he damn well shouldn't have come with her. God, he'd taken a risk. Anyone could have seen him, could have called the police or, worse yet, St. John.

Closing his eyes, he breathed deep, willing that feeling away. He couldn't act on it now; he couldn't rescue her again. But when he opened his eyes, the first thing he noticed was the commotion at the back door of the high-rise apartment building. Two men carried her out, subduing her struggles as they juggled weapons. One of them raised his hand and struck her.

Son of a bitch...

Rage coursed through him, heating his blood. He, who hadn't wanted anyone to die in this war he'd declared, suddenly wouldn't mind killing a man with his bare hands. And that was the only way he'd be able to defend Jillian. As he'd told her earlier, he didn't carry a gun.

Until now, though, he really hadn't needed a gun. He'd only needed a plan and the shadows to conceal his movements. His jaw clenched, and he turned away from the sight of Jillian trying to fight them off. He returned to the shadows, hurrying into the parking garage. The first light of dawn hadn't invaded the concrete structure yet. He would use the dark—and the element of surprise—and hope like hell he wouldn't wind up getting them both killed.

Chapter Eight

Fear gripping her, Jillian fought the men as hard as she could. If only she had a tire iron now…

If only she had *him*…

Her throat burned as she screamed. Swinging her fists and legs, she ignored the stinging in her cheek from the blow she'd received and the pain radiating up her wrists and ankles from the blows she dealt.

One of the men grunted and cursed. "You sure he wants her alive?"

"If we bring her back dead, he doesn't have to know it was us. We can say we found her that way." Unlike the blond guard who'd Jillian recognized from previous attempts to get inside the estate, these men—older and with military buzz cuts—were strangers. But she wondered what she would find on their records were she to investigate them. Assaults. Murders? She'd bet they weren't security guards; they were mercenaries.

"If we kill her," the man with short gray hair pointed out, "St. John won't ever know that she was at Franklin Eberhardt's place."

"If we bring her back to the estate…"

"He'll know you screwed up," Jillian said. "That you left a witness. It was you—you killed him."

She winced as another blow struck her cheek, and a cry of pain slipped through her lips. But then one of the men lifted a gun, pointed the barrel close to her face. Her heart slammed into her ribs, and her eyes burned with tears she refused to shed. She wouldn't beg; pleas for her life would not convince them to spare her.

"Let's just kill her now."

"I wouldn't do that," a raspy voice advised.

Her heart leaped with hope, and like the men who held her, she turned her head to face him. He was so tall; his dark hair almost brushed against the steel beams that held the concrete ceiling above them. And his body was so broad that they could barely see around to the cars parked behind him.

The gray-haired man laughed. "Hell, we're going to be heroes if we kill them both."

"Or martyrs," the raspy voice warned them.

The guy holding her tensed. "What do you mean? You haven't even drawn a gun. You're probably not even carrying one."

"I don't need one," he assured them, his dark gaze meeting hers with a secret message.

But she had no idea what he was trying to tell her. He hadn't shared any of his secrets with her. Hell, she didn't even know his name.

"The only martyr here is you," the gray-haired guy said as he turned the gun on him. "Coming here unarmed…"

"I never said I wasn't armed." The man in the mask opened the palm of his gloved hand. "I don't need a gun," he said. "I've got this."

"A remote control?"

"A kill switch," he said, his voice an ominous rumble. "If you shoot me—if I drop the remote or push this button—the whole damn garage goes up."

"You'll kill her, too," the gray-haired man said.

"Yeah, but you're going to kill her, anyway," Dante reminded them. "This way she won't be going out alone."

The guy holding Jillian dropped her arm and stepped back. "You got this garage wired?"

Beneath the mask her savior's lips curved into a slight grin. "What do you think?"

"I think you're crazy," Jillian said. Why had he come back for her? Why had he risked his life for hers?

"But if you blow this place, you're going to die, too," one of the men said.

He shrugged those impossibly broad shoulders. "I'm already dead."

The guard who stood behind Jillian gasped. Obviously he'd heard the same rumors she had, but he believed the myth.

The masked man, who'd so often been called the phantom, grinned wider. Then he fiddled with the remote, his fingers edging closer to the buttons. "Maybe it's time I had company in hell."

The guy who'd held Jillian whirled around and ran for the exit. His retreat drew the attention of his partner, just long enough that he didn't see the blow coming. A gloved fist connected with his head, knocking him to the pavement. The man in the mask kicked away his gun, then struck him again. Her rescuer grabbed Jillian's hand, pulling her from her shocked trance.

"Don't just stand there," Dante warned her as he began to run, tugging her after him toward the stairwell in the corner of the parking structure.

Shots rang out behind them, striking against the steel door to the stairwell as it slammed closed behind them. He picked up a mop that he found on the landing and jammed the wooden stick through the inside handle of the door.

"We're trapped," she said. "If we go up…"

"We're going down," he said, and instead of tugging her along, he swung her up in his arms. His feet hit the steps hard as he descended into the basement. He darted around crates and tools before finding and pulling open a door that led to another flight of stairs, one that brought them even lower than the basement. He'd brought her back to where he lived underground. She'd heard about the tunnels that ran under the entire city, but until the night before, she'd never been inside them. Dante had, though. He'd obviously been using them to carry out all his attacks on St. John's businesses.

"You were lying about the explosives," she said.

He nodded.

"What if they'd called your bluff? What if they'd shot you?" she asked, wrapping her arms tight around his neck.

"I told them…I'm already dead."

And for the first time she began to wonder… if he really was a phantom.

"WHAT DO YOU MEAN?" St. John asked as he stared at the men he had hired specifically for their lack of conscience. "You couldn't find her or you lost her?"

"We had her," one of the men admitted, his jaw swollen and bruised.

St. John gestured toward his face. "She didn't do that to you."

"He was there," the other guard admitted. "He was wired with a bomb."

"So he threatened what?" St. John asked. "To take everyone out if you shot him?"

The gray-haired guy sighed and nodded.

"You should have shot him," St. John said as he pulled a gun from the center drawer of his desk. He shot one man and then the other. Both of them had been too startled to move. Why had they been surprised?

They'd been there the day before, when he'd shot Eberhardt for refusing to buy back his business. He'd left them to clean up the mess. But they'd only created a bigger one.

He buzzed the intercom. "I have something you need to take care of," he told his recently reinstated chief of security. He'd warned the man not to interrupt even if he heard shots. Maybe he could trust Nick Morris.

But it was good that he hadn't trusted anyone else. *He* may have destroyed most of St. John's enterprises, but there was something the phantom didn't know about, something he wouldn't find. It was time St. John cut his losses and left. But he couldn't do that yet, not when he had something else—someone else—he needed gone first.

Morris stepped inside, no surprise flickering in his eyes as he glanced down at the dead men. "I'll take care of this."

St. John shook his head. "No. I want you to find him—the man with no face—and that reporter. I want them dead."

DAMN IT! DAMN IT TO HELL!

Dante had had to bring her to hell again. For her protection…

But what about his? He'd taken an incredible risk back at the parking garage. If something had happened to him, then St. John would have won. And the man would have no reason to hold on to his insurance anymore.

Dante hadn't just risked his own life. He'd risked…everything. And he still risked it now. With no time to blindfold and bind her, he had to trust that she wouldn't lead the authorities, the media or St. John back to him as soon as he let her go.

But he'd painfully learned long ago to trust no one. He tightened his grip as he carried her through the last stretch of the tunnel to his private rooms.

"You don't have to carry me," she said, her soft body wriggling against his chest. "I can walk."

"You have no shoes," he reminded her. And he couldn't let her walk barefoot underground. Hell, he couldn't let her go anywhere right now.

"I lost them earlier…and I had no time to grab a pair…before they abducted me…." She trembled with fear.

He shook with rage. "They hurt you."

Her hair brushed his neck as she shook her head. "No. I'm fine." But a quaver in her voice belied her claim.

At the door to his private rooms, he clasped her close with one arm while he jammed the key in the lock with his other hand. The rusty hinges creaked as the steel door opened, and he swung her over the threshold and shut the door with his back. He dropped the arm beneath her knees, and she slid down his body, her soft curves molding against him, tensing his muscles.

"You're not fine," he said as he stared down into her face. A bruise along her cheekbone had her pale skin turning red and swelling. He ran his gloved fingertip along her jaw. "You're hurt."

She lifted her hand to her face and touched

her cheek. "It's nothing. I've taken harder hits than this before and survived."

"Who hit you?" he asked, his rage surging back with a protectiveness he had only felt for one other person in his life.

She shook her head. "It was a long time ago."

"So it had nothing to do with your job?" It had been personal; someone she'd cared about, someone she'd trusted, had hurt her.

She expelled a ragged sigh. "I can't deny that I do have a dangerous job, at least lately."

"Then quit it," he suggested, even though he was certain she hadn't taken those harder hits on the job. And he wondered now if what he'd considered ambition and aggression was just her determination to survive.

She laughed. "You'd like that. Then you wouldn't have to worry about me finding out who you really are, *Dante*."

"True," he conceded.

"It's too late," she said, her green eyes bright with knowledge and something else. "I already figured out who you are."

His heart slammed against his ribs. Had he betrayed himself? How had he given himself away? He shook his head. "No. You can't know."

Because if she did, her knowledge risked what he'd given up everything to protect.

JILLIAN DIDN'T HAVE to be able to see his whole face to know she'd stunned him. His shock was evident in the intensity of his dark eyes as he stared down at her, and in the way his big body, so close to hers, tensed. He'd gone to great pains to protect his identity, but he'd risked it to protect her.

"You're my hero," she told him.

"What?"

"You've saved my life," she reminded him. "Not once or twice, but three times." He wouldn't have rescued her that many times if he'd only been using her. St. John was wrong about him. Everyone was wrong about him. He wasn't a phantom or a monster; he was a hero.

He shook his head. "Don't mistake me for something I'm not. I'm no romantic robber, stealing from the rich to give to the poor. I'm nobody's hero."

"You're mine," she insisted. "No one has ever come to my rescue before."

"And you've needed to be rescued?"

She had never told anyone about her childhood. But then she'd been right not to trust her ex-husband or her best friend with her painful secret. She shouldn't have trusted them at all, because while she'd been working, they'd been betraying her. "You don't want to hear my sad story," she warned him, forcing a smile.

His gloved fingertip slid across her bottom lip. "You do this," he said, "no matter what's going on—you manage to smile. I've often wondered what's behind that smile."

She laughed, even as nerves lifted goose bumps on her skin. "Most people figure there's nothing behind it."

"Then most people are idiots. There's no mistaking your intelligence," he said with a heavy sigh.

"You say that as if it worries you."

"It does. You worry me," he said as he stepped back from her and moved closer to the door. "Because if anyone messes up my plan, it'll be you."

She shivered with the loss of contact, just now noticing the damp air. "So everything you're doing—everything you're destroying—

it's been according to some plan that you have?"

He uttered a ragged sigh. "You can't quit your job, because you never stop being a reporter, asking question after question...."

"I think *you* should stop," she advised. "Forget about this plan of yours, whatever it is. Forget about St. John. I'm not the only one in danger."

"I can take care of myself," he said, his lips curving into a slight grin beneath that leather mask.

"You were almost blown up, almost shot," she reminded him. "Sure, you can take care of yourself. But I wasn't talking about you."

He tensed. "Then who?"

"Tabitha St. John," she said, her voice cracking with emotion as she remembered the child's fear. "She's caught up in the middle of this...war between you and her father. She's the one who's going to get hurt."

"Why do you think that? What do you know about that little girl?"

"I know that she's scared. She talked to me at the estate. Her father's so caught up trying to take you down that she's been neglected. She doesn't even think he's her dad anymore."

Jillian's dad had been like that, able to control his violent nature, until something set him off. This mystery man was setting off Tobias St. John every time he destroyed more of the billionaire's dwindling empire.

A muscle twitched along his jaw. "Is that so?"

"Yes." She drew in a bracing breath. "I know what she's going through. To be so young and so scared, to have no one to turn to."

"No one to rescue you?"

She nodded. Her mother had been too afraid to help, no matter how much Jillian had pleaded for her to stop him.

"You were abused as a child?"

Emotion choking her, she could only nod again.

"You think someone's abusing Tabitha?"

"I don't know," she admitted, "but she asked me for help. I want to help her."

"And you think you can do that by stopping me?" he asked.

"I don't know what your plan is," she admitted. "But she's caught in the middle."

"So are you."

"But you've protected me," she reminded him. "You need to protect her, too."

"You have no idea…"

"Then tell me."

He shook his head. "I can't. The only thing I can say is that Tabitha *won't* be hurt."

The determination in his raspy voice and dark eyes eased the tight knot of apprehension in Jillian's chest. She believed him. She couldn't see his face, but she believed that he would protect the child as he had protected her. Trembling with cold and nerves, she crossed the space separating them and lifted her hands to his chest. "You are a hero."

God, he was huge—and hard. Muscles rippled beneath her light touch, and his heart pounded fast, the beat strong enough to lift his chest against her palms. "You have no idea who or what I am," he warned her.

He was right. And she knew she should heed his warning—that she should step back. But she moved closer, pressing her body against the long, heavily muscled length of his. "Tell me," she urged him.

"Give you the scoop you're after?" he asked. "Is that what you're doing, trying to seduce me?" He covered her hands with his gloved ones and pulled them away from his chest.

"I'm trying to thank you," she said. "For saving my life. I know that wasn't part of your plan."

"No," he conceded.

"No matter what else you've done, you couldn't let me get hurt."

"But you did get hurt," he reminded her, lifting his hand to her cheek, his gloved fingers sliding gently over the swollen flesh.

She shivered at the sensation of leather against her skin. But what affected her more than the material was that it was his hand—his big, powerful hand—inside the glove. "I would have been killed," she said, "if not for you. I owe you my life."

"I don't want your gratitude."

Maybe it was the adrenaline coursing through her blood. Maybe it was the thrill of having cheated death. Maybe it was just that she was grateful to him. But she wanted him more than she could remember wanting any other man.

She couldn't even see his face but for the line of his strong jaw, his intense dark eyes and his lips. She reached for him again, lifting her hands to his broad shoulders, sliding them around to the back of his neck so that she could pull down his head to hers.

Rising up on tiptoe, her body pressed tightly against his, she only just reached his chin. She slid her lips across it until he bent lower and covered her mouth with his.

Her pulse quickened, racing more than it had when she'd been in danger. It wasn't adrenaline; it was desire that rushed through her. His mouth devoured her, as if he'd been as hungry for her kiss as she'd been for his. His lips, soft and hard, parted hers.

She gasped at the smooth glide of his tongue across her bottom lip. Her fingers slipped into his hair, the dark strands so silky and thick that they concealed the straps that held the mask to his face. All she had to do to discover his identity was tug on them.

Chapter Nine

Fighting free of the desire gripping him, he reached up and caught her hands, manacling them in one of his. What the hell had he been thinking?

"I wasn't reaching for the mask," she said, her voice soft with a sincerity he dare not trust.

He knew women lied. He had grown up listening to his mother tell lies…to him, to the men she'd conned, but even more to herself. Then his ex…

He couldn't even think about the lies she had told him, how she'd just been after his money. She'd played him like Jillian Drake tried to play him now—for her exclusive. He could not trust her. And he sure as hell shouldn't be kissing her.

"I swear," she persisted, "I was just touching

your hair. It's so soft…like your lips." She rose up on tiptoe again and slid her mouth across his, tasting and teasing him. She was so damn sweet. Her tongue touched the tip of his. She tasted like candy—something sweet but tart, too.

"Jillian…" he murmured against her mouth. He needed to warn her that her efforts were futile; he wasn't about to reveal his secrets to her.

But her tongue flitted into his mouth, and desire coursed through him so powerfully that his body shook from the overwhelming force of his need for her. Lifting her in his arms, he knelt on the edge of the bed and lowered her to the mattress. He needed to pull away, to leave her alone. But she clung to him, arching her sexy body into his. Her breasts pushed against his chest.

His control stretched to the breaking point. But he couldn't let go. He could not make love with her no matter how much his body ached with desire for hers. He released her hands, which she eased between them, trailing her fingers down his chest, her nails dragging across the thin fabric of his shirt.

He pulled back from the sweetness of her

mouth and shook his head, trying to clear it of the passion clouding his judgment. He was not the fool she thought him; she could not seduce him into revealing his secret.

He intended to hold her underground until his plan culminated, but even after it was all over, he still couldn't let her learn the truth. She was too good a reporter and his story too unique for her to not want to divulge it. His was the kind of story that would make her career; it would be picked up nationally. And he'd have no privacy. No escape.

He couldn't escape her now. As he tried to pull away, she wrapped her arms around his waist, clutching at his back to hold him to her. He groaned at the sensation of her soft body pressed tight to his.

She tensed, her green eyes wide with concern. "I'm sorry. You're hurt. I forgot about the other night. The explosion. The blood."

"It wasn't mine." Not all of it. He'd gotten some cuts, but nothing like what had happened to his friend, what should have happened to him instead.

"He was important to you," she said perceptively, "the man who died."

"He was," he admitted, his gut clenching with regret and dread.

"How many people have to get hurt before you stop your war against St. John?"

"Just one more," he said, rage testing his control. "Just him."

"Why do you hate him so much?"

He shook his head, amused by her persistence. "How can I get you to stop asking questions?"

Her lips curved into a tempting smile. "Kiss me."

So he did. And as his mouth covered hers, his control snapped. For the first time since his nightmare had begun, he forgot about it— forgot who he really was and everything he'd lost. He thought only of *her*.

And Jillian stopped thinking entirely. She could only *feel* as Dante lowered his body onto hers. As his lips skimmed down her neck, his fingers dealt with her blouse, deftly unbuttoning it. The silk parted, revealing her bra—the lace so thin, her nipples visibly pushed against the cups. She sucked in a breath when he moved his gloved finger along the edge of her bra, tracing the bare flesh above it before moving his thumb over the nipple that pushed against the lace. She arched her back, wanting—*needing*—more.

She had been so busy, so focused on her career, that she couldn't remember the last time she had made love.

While he continued to tease her nipple through the lace, his other hand slid beneath the back of her blouse and unclasped her bra. Then he pushed down the cups, baring her breasts.

A groan slipped through his lips. He lowered his head, and the leather of his mask rubbed against her skin. His mouth skimmed the curve of her breast, and a moan slipped out of her. His lips trailed across the mound and closed over the distended nipple. His teeth gently nipped and tugged.

Pressure built inside Jillian, winding tight with desire for him. The intensity of her need was almost painful, and a cry slipped from her lips.

He stilled. His voice rough with passion, he asked, "Did I hurt you?"

She shook her head, her hair tangling on his pillow. "Nooo…"

His lips curved into a slight grin, but it faded as he studied her face. "You are so damn beautiful," he murmured, the words sounding like more of a curse than a compliment. "I want to see all of you."

She shivered, suspecting he wasn't talking about just her body. She'd already told him more about her life than she had anyone else. Fortunately, he hadn't pressed her for details. He hadn't asked for more than she was willing to share. But she wanted to share…everything…with him, and she didn't even know his name, couldn't even see his face. But maybe that made it easier. Since she couldn't see him, he couldn't see her, either.

But he stared at her now as he stripped off her skirt, leaving her clad only in her open blouse, hanging, unclasped bra and black lace panties. He groaned. "So damn beautiful…"

And vulnerable. She was nearly naked while he remained fully clothed. Except for the gloves he now stripped off. "I have to touch you," he said. His hands slid over her, his skin rough as if chapped and scarred. "I have to feel you…."

He left on the mask and answered the plea she hadn't been able to voice. Pushing aside her panties, he kissed her intimately, his tongue flicking over the nub of her desire before dipping inside her. The leather mask rubbed against her, adding to the eroticism.

She squirmed, the pressure so intense that a moan slipped from her throat.

His groan echoed it as he feasted on her body. His tongue moved in and out of her with delicious friction.

"Oh!" The spiral started, the free fall into pleasure.

His bare hands moved up her body, cupping her breasts, his thumbs teasing her nipples as he continued to make love to her with his mouth. His lips sucked. His tongue stroked.

Her body shuddered, and a scream tore from her throat at the intensity, at the never-ending pleasure that rippled through her.

"Jillian…" He sighed.

Her body humming with satisfaction, Jillian closed her eyes and just barely resisted the urge to purr as she shifted on the tangled sheets.

"You're not going to sleep," he warned her as he kissed his way back up her body.

Passion stirred again as he tugged at first one nipple, then the other.

"We're not done," she promised him. Not

when he touched her like that. He only made her greedy for more.

Her hands trembling, she pushed his coat from his shoulders. It fell to the floor with a ping. Something metal must have fallen from the wool, a button, perhaps. She forgot about it as she lifted his T-shirt, rolling the cotton up over the washboard abs of his stomach. His hands covered hers, pulling them away. He pulled the shirt off for her, dragging it up his chest and over his head.

A gasp slipped through her lips—at the masculine perfection of his body and the scratches and gouges that marred his smooth flesh. "You *are* hurt."

"I'm hurting now," he said, his voice a raspy whisper. "I'm hurting for you…."

Her hands skimmed gently over his chest, avoiding the ridges of dried blood on the deep scratches. His skin was as smooth and supple beneath her palms and as rich in texture as the leather of his mask. Then she moved her hand lower, over his rippling abs, to the snap of his jeans. "Then take me…"

He caught her fingers in a tight grasp. "Are you playing games with me, Jillian?"

"I'm not playing any games," she insisted,

but she wished that she was, that her attraction to him was only a ploy to gain his confidence and discover his identity. How could she be so attracted to a man she didn't know or trust?

"I won't stop you again," he warned her as he unsnapped and pushed his jeans down his legs. "You better make sure this is what you want…."

His thighs were as heavily muscled as his chest and arms. And the rest of him…

"I want you. I won't change my mind."

He kissed her deeply, sliding his tongue in and out of her mouth. And as he kissed her, he finished undressing her, pulling her unbuttoned blouse and unclasped bra from her shoulders.

Cool air rushed over her back. Then his hands were there, sliding over her bare skin as he pulled her tightly against him. Jillian arched into him, pushing her breasts against the silky skin of his muscular chest. A moan burned in her throat. His lips skimmed across her cheek, to her ear, then her throat. He suckled at her madly beating pulse. Then his hands moved, too, from her back to her hips, and he slid down the last bit of lace that covered her.

Lifting her, he wrapped her legs around his waist.

The sensitive skin of her inner thighs rubbed against his hard muscles. She clenched him, but he slid her up his body. His hands stroked over her breasts. Her nipples pushed against his palms as she arched again, whimpering for his touch. For him to release the pressure that built unbearably inside her.

He lifted her higher, bringing her breasts level with his mouth. Leather brushed against her skin as he skimmed his lips over the mounds.

She clenched his shoulders, her nails nipping into the broad expanse of muscle, as his teeth nipped her skin. Then his tongue soothed over the love bite. She moaned, wanting more. *Needing* more.

And he gave her more. He tugged a nipple into his mouth, his tongue teasing the aching peak. Sliding over and over the sensitive point. He knew exactly where and how to touch her. He *knew* her as no one else ever really had.

She locked her legs behind his back and arched against him, moaning. "Please…"

Foil tore as he sheathed himself, then he pulled her down onto his erection. She arched her hips, stretching to accept him. But he was so big…so overwhelmingly big.

"You're so tight," he murmured, his jaw clenched, his teeth gritted, as he eased inside her. "And hot…"

Passion burned deep within her. Jillian's body had never been filled the way he filled her—stretching her taut, touching her more deeply than she'd ever been touched. She locked her legs behind his back, holding on as he began to thrust in and out of her.

His hands joined hers on the headboard, locking around the rails above her fingers. The brass bed rattled as they found a frantic rhythm, each of them racing to release the pressure that threatened to shatter their bodies. Stars danced behind Jillian's eyelids as pleasure exploded inside her body.

He thrust harder, intensifying that pleasure until she screamed. Then his cry—a primal cry of release—joined the echo of her scream as he filled her with his hot passion. She'd known he was a powerful man from the minute he had grabbed her off the street, but she'd never suspected the power of the emotions he would be able to draw from her. He'd rescued her time and time again, putting himself in danger to save her. And now he'd saved her again, from locking her feelings away behind the wall she'd built up to protect herself from hurt. Warmth flooded her chest, and her pulse pounded with a terrifying realization.

Could she actually be falling for her mystery lover?

FRUSTRATION POUNDED inside his head and pulsed in every muscle of his body. Dante had found a greater release than he'd ever known in her arms. But it hadn't changed a thing. If anything, it had only reminded him more of all that he'd lost.

He hadn't even been able to disclose his identity to the woman in his bed, in his arms. The woman who slept now in sheets tangled from their lovemaking. But he'd left her there, locked in his private rooms. And now he had to forget about her; he had to focus on the plan. But that proved hard when he could feel her on his skin, taste her on his lips. When he couldn't stop wanting her…

"Today we'll hit St. John's private airfield," he announced to the *soldiers* gathered in the annex of the underground tunnels, "disabling the planes and the helicopter." And making sure St. John couldn't escape. "Then after that mission is complete, we'll take out the power station and jam the satellite receivers."

"The power station?" one of the soldiers echoed, his voice bouncing off the cement walls of the annex.

"We have to shut down the city," he explained. "No electricity. No communication." Because tonight, when the entire city was dark, the man with no face intended to take back his life.

"But we'll cripple the city," someone murmured.

"We'll cripple St. John," Sergeant Wallace replied for him with a sideways glance at his mask. Like the man who'd died in the explosion, Wallace was aware of his true identity. Only the ones with whom Dante had served in the Special Forces had been trusted with his secret. They'd enlisted the others to help, paying them with booty from the break-ins. But his friends knew this was about so much more than money.

"What if he knows it's us?" a young man whispered, his voice squeaky with fear.

He knows.

"St. John will not have the means to come after us," he assured his men, "not once we're done with him. The plan will work," he promised his soldiers. And himself. The plan had to work....

"What about the reporter?" the sergeant asked.

What about her? He could not think about Jillian, could not let her back into his head. And never into his heart. He would not let her interfere with his plan. He had to remind himself that it was all a ploy. She had just been manipulating him, trying to con him into giving her the story that would make her career. He knew better than to trust anyone other than these men. And they had to trust him. "I have locked her in my private room. She won't be a problem," he assured his men.

Doubt flickered in the eyes of the sergeant. "But if she were to escape before our missions..." Wallace said. "If she were to tell someone...if she were to tell St. John..."

He shook his head in reply to the question in his old friend's eyes. He hadn't revealed his identity to her. "She won't escape. And even if she did, she wouldn't tell." He hoped.

"But she's an investigative reporter," Wallace persisted. "She has a reputation for being relentless when she goes after a story. You can't trust her."

"I don't trust her," he assured the older man as well as the others. "And because I don't, I won't be letting Jillian Drake go *anywhere*." Not until his ultimate mission was accomplished. "She won't be a problem."

Even as he uttered the words, he recognized the lie. She was already a problem. Then he noticed a shadow on the wall of the annex; the curves and wavy hair did not belong to one of his soldiers.

Jillian had awakened and somehow escaped. Now he had to catch her before she ruined everything.

FEAR PARALYZED JILLIAN. He was going to kill her. If he found her…

Wasn't that what he'd meant…? She wasn't going to be a problem. He wasn't letting her go.

She'd awakened, naked and satiated, only to find herself alone in bed. The door locked. Fortunately she'd stepped on the key that had dropped from his coat when she'd pushed it from his shoulders. When she'd made love with him…with a man who intended to hold her hostage or worse…

Tears of regret and shame stung her eyes. She had the worst judgment; she always put her trust in the wrong people. Every time she let herself begin to care about someone she got hurt. *Damn…*

She blinked back the tears, refusing to give in to self-pity. She had to move; she had to find her way out of the sewers, had to make her way back to civilization. The tunnel from his private rooms had led her here, to where all the tunnels converged. Coming upon the group of men, she had crouched down, hiding herself behind rows of metal barrels. They hadn't seen her because all of their attention had been focused on him.

They had hung on his every word, and so had she. Was this community of people living in the sewers some kind of criminal cult, and he was their leader?

She had made love with this mystery man, with this beast. She'd been such a fool. Again. But this time the man she'd trusted wasn't going to just take her heart; he was going to take her life.

Careful to draw no attention to herself, she moved cautiously, rising slightly to peer around the barrels. But the light was too dim for her to get a good look at the men who'd gathered around him; she could only see the torches that flickered in the annex, casting shadows against the rough cement walls. The sewers were old, the tunnels nearly as crude as caves.

How could anyone live down here? More importantly, *why* would anyone? Because they were hiding from something or someone. That had to be why he wore his mask, too. Was he that wanted? That bad a man? Was he a killer?

He had promised her that Tabitha wouldn't be hurt. But his plan was to destroy Tobias St. John. She doubted he would care if a child was hurt in the cross fire of the war he waged.

For what? Money? Possessions?

She ducked back behind the barrels. Her elbow brushed against one, and it teetered from where it perched precariously atop the others. She held her breath, waiting for it to fall and draw attention to her hiding place.

But a gloved hand touched the barrel, steadying it. Her gaze traveled from his hand, up his heavily muscled arm, to his broad shoulder and then his face. His very angry face.

Because of the mask, she could see only the line of his mouth, his eyes. But she saw his anger in the tautness of his strong jaw and the intensity of his dark gaze.

Trapped in the depths of his gaze, she didn't doubt that she'd misinterpreted what he'd told his men. Even though he had made love with her, he would kill her before he'd let her go again.

Chapter Ten

Pulling the key from his pocket, St. John breathed a sigh of relief. It didn't matter what the masked man had done, what he had destroyed. He couldn't have touched this. The locker, in the crowded bus terminal, was undisturbed. The lock secure, clicking open only after he slid the key inside the tumblers.

The phantom didn't know about this—about the money, the gold and the stocks that St. John had hidden away. His hand shaking in anticipation, he lifted the handle and opened the locker.

The empty locker.

Son of a bitch...

How had he known? How had he found this, too? Did they have some damn special connection? How could they, when he hadn't even known St. John existed?

Now it was too late for St. John. Rage coursing through him, he slammed the metal door with such force that it bounced back open. And he realized it wasn't empty.

The folded paper on the bottom of it was no bomb. *He* wouldn't have wired the locker with a bomb; he wouldn't have wanted to endanger any innocent people in the bus depot. But even knowing that, St. John's hand trembled as he reached for the note. In addition to a map and a meeting time, handwriting eerily similar to his own spelled out the terms of an exchange. "I have what you want. You have what I want."

It wasn't that simple. How did his enemy not know that? How did he not understand that St. John didn't want to just take what mattered most to him, he wanted everything—including the man's life.

Only then would St. John be satisfied.

"ARE YOU GOING to kill me?" she asked as he carried her through the doorway into his private rooms. He kicked the door shut behind him, but it wouldn't matter if he locked it—not if she still had the key she'd used for her escape.

"Answer me!" she demanded, but her voice quavered with fear.

He shook his head, disgusted with himself and her. "I don't have to kill you—you're going to get yourself killed. St. John's men want you dead. If you leave here, they're going to kill you for sure. And I won't be around to help you." Not once night fell; he had a very special meeting to attend.

"I heard you…what you told your men," she said, her breath hitching. "That you're not letting me leave here, that I won't be a problem…"

Yet she hadn't fought him back in the annex. She hadn't resisted when he'd closed his arms around her and picked her up. He'd been relieved, as he was too tired and distracted to fight with her.

"If you heard that, then you heard the plan, too," he said with a weary sigh.

Her eyes wide with fear and confusion, she nodded.

"I can't let you interfere with that plan." He had to make damn sure she didn't get away again.

"You've never told me why you're going after St. John," she said, her green eyes narrowed with suspicion and confusion. "Why?"

Anger and impatience sharpening the tone of his voice, he told her, "It's none of your concern."

He did not have time to explain things to her; he didn't have time for her at all. But yet he was stuck here, in the sewer, until night fell. Until the power was cut and St. John's escape route blocked.

"Do you know how crazy it was to try to escape?" St. John had a kill-on-sight order out on her. And him.

She shrank away from him, as if she actually believed he would hurt her, even after they'd been as intimate as two people could be. His bare hands shaking slightly, he reached for her. But she stepped back.

"Jillian…" Regret tugged at him, soothing his anger. He hadn't wanted to scare her.

Then she moved again, flying at him. She pummeled his chest with her fists and kicked at his legs.

"Damn it, woman!"

But as angry as she made him, he would much rather see her like this—fighting—than cowering with fear. He lifted and tossed her onto the bed. And before she could roll off the mattress, he covered her. The weight of his body stifled the movement of her limbs. She couldn't fight; she could only arch her body into his. Her breasts pushed against his chest. Her hips ground against his erection.

He uttered a groan of desire at the contact. "Jillian, stop fighting me…."

"I'm not going to make it easy for you," she said, wriggling beneath him.

She hadn't made anything easy for him since he had first grabbed her in front of that exploding building. Hell, maybe he should have left her up there with the real monster.

"The one you're making it hard for is yourself," he cautioned her. She was making him hard, too, with all her squirming.

God, the woman drove him insane….

Jillian shivered in his arms. She was both scared and excited. His hard body betrayed his passion for her while his eyes still burned with anger and frustration.

His hands rough with impatience, he covered her body, checking the shallow pockets of her skirt. Not satisfied that he'd searched thoroughly enough, he unclasped the skirt and dragged it off her, shaking out the material before dropping it onto the floor. "Where is it?"

"What?" she asked, even though she knew.

"Where's the damn key?"

"You're going to have to find it yourself," she taunted him.

His eyes gleamed. "Gladly." And he reached for the buttons on her blouse, tugging them free. Then he pulled the blouse from her shoulders and tossed it onto the floor. "No key."

She shook her head. "No key."

She could have lied and told him she had dropped it somewhere in the tunnels. But no matter what she'd heard him tell his army, she wanted him to keep looking, to keep touching her. Because his touch told her more than his words. He wanted her too much to hurt her.

His gaze, hot with desire, traveled the length of her body, from her toes up to her eyes, lingering on the curves in between that were covered, but only with thin black lace. "Where could you be hiding that key?"

She bit her bottom lip, passion igniting inside her from just the heat of his gaze. Her legs shifted as she rubbed her thighs together, tension building. A tension only *he* could relieve.

He groaned, then ordered, "Damn it, give me the key, Jillian!"

She wouldn't blindly obey him like his other followers. She shook her head.

Sliding his hands beneath her back, he unclipped her bra and slid the straps from her shoulders. As he dropped the lace onto the floor atop her clothes, he chuckled, and his dark eyes glittered with triumph. His fingertip flicked over metal, where the key nestled between her breasts. But he didn't pick it up. Yet. Instead, he leaned forward, nuzzling her breasts with the leather mask, and lifted the key from between her breasts with his teeth. Cold metal grazed her sensitive skin.

At the erotic sensation, a moan slipped from between her lips. "Ohhh…"

He teased her again with the key, pressing the metal against her nipple.

She arched beneath him. "Please…"

Disappointment filled her when he pocketed the key. He had what he wanted. So he probably intended to leave her locked inside the windowless room. But he stared down at her, his gaze intense—and conflicted.

"Damn you," he groaned, cursing her even as he lowered his mouth to hers. His kiss was hard, punishing.

She parted her lips for the bold invasion of his tongue, moaning as it slid inside her mouth. He tasted dark and rich—and as mysterious as the face he hid behind a mask. He pulled away and tore off all of his clothes—everything but that leather mask. And she trembled again, not in fear but in anticipation of the pleasure she knew only her mystery lover could bring her.

He made love to her with a passion she'd never felt before—*from* a man or *for* a man. But along with desire, she sensed desperation in them both. His plan was dangerous; he'd nearly died once executing it. He had to be as aware of the risks as she was.

But as he thrust deep inside her—to her very core—she was aware of another risk, of falling for this mysterious stranger. He kissed her lips, her throat, the curve of her breasts… edging her closer to release from the pressure building inside her. Then he moved again, rolling onto his back so that she straddled him, and sank deeper inside her. Pleasure so intense that she screamed crashed over her. But he held her hips, driving deep until she shattered with ecstasy. With a guttural groan, he joined her.

"I thought you were going to kill me," she said as she curled into his shoulder. Satiated and secure, she pressed a kiss against his chest where his heart pounded hard.

He stroked a hand down her side, over the curve of her hip. "I never said that."

"But you implied it," she pointed out, "when you were talking to your men. You told them a lot of things."

His arm tightened around her. "You shouldn't have been eavesdropping."

"Sometimes it's the only way I can learn things," she admitted. "What's going on? Why did you order those attacks on his airfield? And the power station? You're going to cause a citywide blackout."

He expelled a ragged sigh. "I'm not going to give you a story, Ms. Drake."

A smile tugged at her mouth over his reverting to using her surname…after what they had just done.

"I don't want a story anymore," she

admitted, surprising even herself. "I don't want to be here, but you won't let me go."

"I can't."

She understood that, too. She was safer in here, with him, than she would be out there alone. Even as scared as she'd been when she had overheard what he'd told his men, she'd instinctively known that. That was why she hadn't fought him when he'd found her. While he refused to admit it, he was protecting her. From St. John and maybe from being caught in the cross fire of his plan.

"You're sure Tabitha won't be hurt?" she asked, fear for the child knotting her stomach. "You're sure she'll be safe during the blackout?" As a kid, she'd been terrified of the dark. But she'd forced herself to face that fear, as she'd faced so many others.

"I'd die before I'd let any harm come to her," he said, his voice rough with emotion.

Jillian shivered at the intensity of his claim. "You know her, don't you? But then you must—this thing between you and St. John, it's personal."

He didn't reply, but that muscle twitched along his jaw again.

"How do you know him?" she asked. She'd

checked into St. John's background, but had found no mention of anyone like her mystery lover. A dark-haired giant of a man hadn't been on his list of enemies or friends. "When did you two meet?"

"Give it up," he warned her.

As she lifted her head from his chest to study him, she noted the tattoo on his arm, an eagle with the words *Semper Fi* beneath his wings. "You were a marine, too. Is that how you know him?"

"I'm not telling you any of my secrets, Ms. Drake, so you might as well get some sleep," he advised her, stroking his hand down her side again. "Maybe by the time you wake up, it'll all be over."

She tensed in his arms. "You're leaving, then?" She wasn't the only one in danger. St. John had to want him dead a lot more than he wanted her dead.

"Not yet," he said. "I have a few hours before dark. A few hours to sleep. I won't be distracted again."

"Have I distracted you?" she asked, suspecting he wasn't referring to just her questions.

That slight grin curved his lips again. "You know you have."

"Has saving me or seducing me been the distraction?" she teased.

Beneath the mask, his grin widened. "I'm not sure who seduced whom anymore."

Neither was she. But she had no doubt that he had saved her.

"I won't distract you again," she promised. Because he had rescued her so many times, she owed him that much, even though she didn't understand what he was doing or why.

He sighed. "If only that were true..."

Jillian dropped her head back onto his shoulder and lay quietly in his arms, unwilling to distract him anymore. But she was too frightened to close her eyes. Not only would she see Tabitha silently pleading for help, but she might see Dante—what she feared would happen to him when he took on St. John again. This time he might be the one getting zipped into a body bag.

Why was he willing to risk his life to destroy Tobias St. John? What had the man done to him? All those questions burned in her mind, but she kept them from leaving her lips.

He needed sleep for the mission he had

planned that evening. Finally he succumbed, his dark lashes brushing against the eyeholes in the mask as his eyes shut.

Who was he, this man she was beginning to fall for? A hero or a villain? A knight in slightly tarnished armor or a ruthless killer?

It wasn't the reporter in her who had to know. It was the woman, the woman who feared she had fallen in love with another man unworthy of her trust.

Fingers trembling, she reached for the straps at the back of his head. She held her breath as she fumbled with the snaps. The metal emitted a soft click with each release. And she stilled, watching those eyeholes, checking to see if he watched her.

But he didn't move. Until she lifted the leather from his face. Then he met her startled gaze.

"No…"

He couldn't be. She could not have just made love—not once but twice—with Tobias St. John.

Chapter Eleven

Her green eyes wide with shock, she murmured, "You're not a monster."

"I'm not so sure about that." She didn't sound all that certain, either, he noticed.

Tobias rubbed his hand over his naked face. He had worn the mask for so long that it had nearly become a part of him. His skin tingled as air rushed over it.

Since the mask was gone, his secret out, he lifted the contacts from his irises. He hadn't needed them as anything but a disguise. A disguise he'd hated wearing. Maybe that was why he hadn't stopped her when he'd felt her fumbling with the straps—because he'd wanted it off. Maybe that was why he wasn't mad that she'd gone for it the minute she'd thought him asleep. He should have been furious, but he was only disappointed that he'd been right not to trust her.

"Your eyes…" Jillian gasped as he met her gaze. "You really are Tobias St. John."

At this point, he wasn't sure who he was anymore, so he said nothing.

She shook her head as her eyes filled with horror; apparently she would have rather slept with a faceless monster than him. "But how…" she sputtered. "How could you be in two places at once? Up there and down here? Is there a tunnel under the estate?"

"I haven't been in two places at once," he said. But he had been careful to conceal his identity so that no one would suspect that the man who claimed to be him was actually an imposter.

"But you were at the police station," she said. "They called you there when they were holding me.…"

He shook his head. "It wasn't me."

"At your house…"

"It wasn't me."

"I don't understand." Her brow furrowed in confusion. "I've done an extensive background check on you. I know you don't have any family. And no one could get plastic surgery that good that would fool so many people."

Nearly everyone. But his daughter. Thank God Tabitha had never believed that monster was her daddy.

"Get dressed," he said as he rolled out of bed himself. Sleeping had been impossible even before she'd pulled off his mask. He was too close to rest now. And she was too close. She'd figure out everything soon enough.

"I don't understand," she repeated. "Why would *you* want to live like this?"

"You think I want to be down here?" he asked. "You think I want to live like this?" He reached for the mask, taking it from her slack grip. He had to put it back on; not everyone in his underground army knew his real identity. So he had to wear the thing a little while longer—until the exchange, until Tabitha was safely back in his arms.

He jerked his clothes on, impatient for night to come. Making love with Jillian Drake hadn't relieved any of his tension; it had only added to it. If he'd locked her in the room alone...

If he'd walked away from her...

He watched with regret as she covered her

curves and alabaster skin. She was too beautiful for him to ignore or forget. Her fingers trembled on the buttons of her blouse and the clasp of her skirt. "Are you going to let me go now?" she asked.

He chuckled, albeit with no humor. "That's even less of a possibility now than it was before."

"Because I know too much? Because I know who you are?"

"You don't know anything," he said as he put the contacts back in his eyes and fastened the mask back onto his face. She was as ignorant as he had once been. He unlocked and opened the door.

If she was smart, she would have run from him. But instead, she followed where he led her down the tunnel, to another secret room. The door was unlocked, but guards sat inside, staring at a wall of monitors playing security footage.

She gasped. "It looks like the editing room at the station."

The guards gasped, too, with surprise at her intrusion. They glanced from her to Tobias. He nodded, silently assuring them that it was okay that she was here. That he had everything under control. But he wasn't foolish enough to really believe he could control Jillian Drake.

"But the screens in your editing room are showing stuff that already happened," Anthony, the young computer expert, remarked. "This is playing out now. Live." He'd hacked into the security system at the estate, a system Tobias had just had installed before the imposter had taken over his life. But the system hadn't been as high-tech as Tobias had thought; the kid had breached it with no trouble, allowing them access to the entire estate.

On one of the screens, the imposter sat in Tobias's den, behind Tobias's desk, drinking Tobias's whiskey. The only comfort Tobias had was that it looked as if the man really needed the drink. Stubble darkened his jaw; his hair was mussed, as if he'd been running his hands through it. He looked like a man with few options left. Actually, although he didn't know it yet, he only had one.

But yet the bastard struggled to accept that, struggled to accept that he wasn't as smart and powerful as he'd believed he was.

"That's him," she murmured. "That's…"

He caught her before she could reveal anything, jerking her closer to his side. Then he turned to his men. "Take a break. I can handle it for a minute."

"With her?" one of them questioned. "You trust her?"

When she'd taken off his mask, she hadn't left him much choice. "Yes." But even as he made the admission, he recognized it for the lie it was. He wasn't really capable of trusting anyone.

She waited until the men left the room, shutting the door behind them, before she turned from her intense scrutiny of those monitors and focused on him. "They claim this is a live feed. But how do I know they're telling the truth? How do I know *you're* telling the truth?"

"That's why I brought you here," he explained. Although he wasn't sure he understood his need for her to know that *he* wasn't the imposter. He'd hoped no one, besides those who already knew, would learn the truth. But now...

JILLIAN BLINKED, unable to focus on the monitors before her, unable to accept what he claimed. She gestured toward all those security screens and said, "This proves nothing."

"Just watch," he advised as he clicked some buttons on a keyboard.

One of the screens changed to an image she recognized: Vicky's young face flushed with nerves and pinched with concern. Then volume played through speakers mounted on the cement walls. "This is a live broadcast from Channel 13, WXXM. Investigative reporter Jillian Drake disappeared last night. Her car was recovered from the scene of the explosion that went off in the industrial area of River City just before dawn. While her car was badly burned, it was determined there was nobody in the vehicle. Authorities are searching for Jillian Drake. But if anyone has any information about her whereabouts, they should contact Channel 13 directly."

"St. John—" she turned to him "—*you* bought WXXM."

"I didn't buy the station, and neither did he." He tapped the screen that showed the image of him, drinking at his desk. With a click on the keyboard, the camera turned at an angle so that a television screen was visible inside the room; Vicky's mouth was moving as she continued to report from the scene of Jillian's disappearance.

"Oh, my God! So he's really there…and you're really here," she said, her shock and confusion returning with a throbbing headache. "But that doesn't tell me which one of you is the real Tobias St. John."

"I don't have to tell you," he said. And she worried he was going back to keeping his secrets, but then he reminded her, "Tabitha told you."

He's not my daddy.…

She shivered with the realization that the little girl had been right. "Tabitha—she's *your* daughter."

"And I'm her daddy," he said, his voice cracking with emotion.

He'd betrayed that emotion before when he'd talked about the child, revealing that he'd had a connection to Tabitha St. John. Now Jillian understood exactly how deep their connection was.

"But I don't understand," she said, hating that she kept repeating that phrase. "Why are you down here, and that…that…"

"Imposter," he supplied the word, his voice rough with disgust.

"Imposter is in your house?" Relief eased some of her confusion; that man who'd been so threatening and creepy hadn't really been Tobias. That was why she'd been so disappointed that he wasn't the man she'd been drawn to these past three years. He hadn't been the myth or the man. At least, not the real one. "Even before Tabitha said anything to me, I knew something was strange about him—when he let me onto the estate, when he agreed to speak to me."

"I would have never done that," he agreed.

"Why not?" she asked. "Why did you never grant me an interview?"

"I value my privacy, Ms. Drake."

Jillian gestured at the rough cement walls of the tunnel and then at his leather mask. "Isn't this a bit extreme to protect it?"

"It's not my *privacy* I'm trying to protect now." A muscle twitched in his cheek as he clenched his jaw.

"Tabitha," she whispered. "How can you protect her from here? By leaving her with him?"

"You think I left her there?" His voice finally rose above that raspy whisper to a shout, and she recognized the distinctive deep tone of it. "You think I had a choice?"

"So he's taken her hostage?" she asked, fear gripping her. That poor little girl…

His jaw rigid with anger, he nodded.

"He's the one who killed her nanny," she realized. "And the other woman?"

"She must have been the nanny the agency sent to replace Mindy," he replied.

"So the woman who's there now is a fraud," she said. Jillian had suspected Susan wasn't a real nanny, and that the blonde had seemed too close to St. John to have only known him a couple of weeks. "She's in on the kidnapping with him."

He jerked his chin in a sharp nod. That rigid jaw, his massive build, the very magnetism of Tobias St. John's larger-than-life personality—it was all there, enhanced by the mask instead of concealed. How could she have missed it?

Disgusted with herself, she shook her head. "I should have known…I should have known you were *you*." Because she'd been drawn to him, just as she had before the imposter had assumed his life.

"I'm not *me*," he said, and the disgust was all his now. "I'm nobody right now. I'm that phantom your witnesses called me. A shadow of my former self. Like you said, Dante…"

In hell because of an imposter.

"But who is *he?*" she wondered. "How did he just…"

"Take over my life?" He stared up at the monitor, at the image of himself.

"That can't be just the result of plastic surgery," she said. "He doesn't just look exactly like you. He sounds like you. He acts like you."

"No." That muscle jumped in his cheek again. "He doesn't act like me."

She lifted her shoulders in a shrug. "He fooled me. He's fooled everyone. Your security force. The police."

"None of them, especially you, really know me," he pointed out. "He didn't fool everyone, though. He didn't fool the people who matter."

Jillian's breath caught over the little twinge of pain his words caused her. She'd made love with him, but she didn't matter. She should have expected as much. She'd never mattered to anyone.

"Who is he?" she asked again, forcing herself to focus. "Over the three years since I started working at WXXM, I ran all kinds of background checks on you. I didn't find any relatives but Tabitha."

"That's what I thought, too." He expelled a ragged sigh as he studied that man on the screen. "God, I wish that was really the case."

"But it's not."

"I don't have time for this," he said with a groan of frustration.

"I thought you had no place to be until dark."

"I'm still not going to grant you an interview," he said. "You know as much as you need to know."

"And more than you wanted me to know," she surmised. "But I don't know enough to understand any of it."

"Why do you need to?"

"Because I care," she admitted, her voice cracking with emotion. God, she had begun to fall for him. "I care about Tabitha."

"You only talked to her once," he reminded her.

But the child's fear had touched her and had brought back all Jillian's old fears and helplessness. "She asked me to help her then. And I want to help."

"I have it under control."

"You want me under control," she said. It was probably why he'd made love to her, so she would lose her objectivity, which she had. "I swear—whatever you tell me, it's off the record. I won't report it."

"Have you ever given that off-the-record line and actually meant it?" he asked.

"I only say what I mean."

He sighed. "So what do you want to know?"

"How did this happen?"

"I had a mother until I was twelve," he said, his deep voice curiously devoid of emotion. "Then social services deemed her unfit, took me away from her and put me in foster care. She never called, never tried to see me. I figured she was dead until she called me a few weeks ago. She had something to tell me, but I didn't give her the chance."

Jillian understood his unwillingness. Had

her father ever called her, she wouldn't have talked to him, either.

"I figured she just wanted some money," he explained. "Then she died, leaving me listed as her next of kin. So I had to go back to Detroit to handle the funeral arrangements, and while I was gone, I got a call from my head of security. He warned me that someone was pretending to be me."

Tobias flinched at the understatement. The man was more than pretending; he'd stolen his life from him.

"Someone? Who is he?" she asked.

He couldn't trust that the reporter would really keep everything he told her off the record. But he found himself wanting to share the nightmare he'd been living with the woman who'd become his lover. He wanted her to understand why he'd done everything that he had.

So he replied, "Apparently *he* was what my mother wanted to tell me about." To warn him about, he suspected now. "I wasn't the only one she gave birth to in a crack house thirty-five years ago—I had a brother. A twin. But she didn't keep him."

This was information Jillian wouldn't have

found, no matter how good an investigative reporter she was. He hadn't even had a birth certificate until he'd been put into the foster care system. The name used for his mother hadn't even been her real one.

Her green eyes warmed with sympathy. "And I thought I had a terrible childhood."

He shrugged. He hadn't wanted her pity. "I don't know what happened to him. But for me, it got better. It got good, actually. When I was twelve, I was placed in a foster home with a really nice family."

A normal family, but of course he hadn't realized that at the time. He'd never known normal before. Then it was all he'd wanted to provide for Tabitha; that was why he'd given his ex the money she'd wanted, to protect his little girl from her mother's indifference and selfishness. But he'd failed his daughter.

"You didn't remember him?" Jillian asked.

"I couldn't have been very old—maybe hours—when she sold him."

"Sold him?" Her eyes widened with shock.

Tobias nodded. "That's what he told me. She sold him to a dealer for drugs. The dealer sold him to someone else. He didn't say much more than that."

"So you talked to him?"

"After Morris called me, he—Edward—called and warned me that if I tried coming home, he'd kill Tabitha." Horror clutched at him with fear for his daughter's life. "Said if I showed myself around River City, if I did anything that caused anyone to even suspect that he wasn't me, he would kill Tabitha."

"That's why you didn't call the cops."

He expelled a ragged sigh. "I couldn't take the risk."

"But leaving her there…?"

He tapped the keyboard again, bringing up another camera view—this one of his little girl sitting in the middle of her bed playing with a doll. Her black hair tangled around her shoulders as if no one had brushed it, and she wore the pajamas she'd worn since she'd awakened.

"You can watch her."

He spent much of his time in front of this monitor, watching over his baby and hoping she could sense his protection. But it wasn't enough. He wanted to hold her and calm her fears. "Yeah."

She reached out and squeezed his arm as if she knew his pain, as if she felt it, too. "You can see if she's in danger, but how do you get there…"

"Before it's too late?" His heart clenched at the possibility. "That's the problem. Even with Morris there, there're too many other guards."

She shuddered. "Like the ones who grabbed me. The mercenaries. Morris wouldn't be able to fight them all off alone."

"No. But he could get her out of immediate danger, at least for a little while." He lifted his fingertip to the screen and pointed at the closet doors. "In the back is a dummy panel that slides open to a secret room. A safe room."

"But Morris will have to be able to get her past the nanny to get to it?"

He nodded. "And she's working with Edward," he said. "Mindy, Tabitha's real nanny, was killed in the park the day I left for Detroit. Morris had an agency send someone else over, but Edward must have intercepted her, too."

Edward had killed anyone who'd gotten in his way, even his own mother. During their phone conversation, the madman had taken great pride in claiming responsibility for her murder. Of course, Edward hadn't actually known her since she'd sold him as an infant. He hadn't spent his life tracking down his biological mother for a reunion, but for revenge. She'd failed him, just as she had failed Tobias—again—when she'd told Edward about him.

She shivered and nodded. "So Morris has to get Tabitha past Susan and Edward? He's the only one who can get her into that secret room?"

"He's the only one who knows about it. It's new." Tobias had installed it after his mother called because just hearing her voice on the phone had brought back all those old memories of the horrible people, drug dealers and criminals, that she'd brought into his life. His childhood fears had reinforced his vow to protect his daughter. Somehow he'd instinctively known his mother would bring someone horrible into their lives again. "It's not stocked. They wouldn't be able to hide in there for very long. So we had to work out a plan."

"Your plan," she said, her brow furrowing with confusion again. "The thefts, the explosions… You're destroying everything that you spent your life building."

"I built nothing. The money and the power and the possessions don't mean anything. All I want is my daughter," he said. "I don't care about anything else."

But Edward did. Tobias didn't have to have grown up with him to know that *only* money and power mattered to the man. People—human life—meant *nothing* to him.

"I didn't destroy everything," he admitted. "I kept enough to persuade him to agree to an exchange—what's left of my money and my meaningless possessions for my daughter."

"How are you going to make the exchange?" she asked. "He's dangerous. You can't trust him."

He snorted. "Of course I can't trust him. But I can distract him."

She nodded. "The power outage. The airfield. Do you think it's enough?"

"It has to be." His plan had already taken two interminable weeks to carry out. But he'd known Edward wouldn't be ready to deal until he had nothing else left. Tobias focused on the view of the camera in the den.

Edward stood and hurled his drink across

the room. The glass shattered as it struck the wall.

"What—what happened?" Jillian asked.

Tobias struck the key, turning up the volume on the news broadcast that Edward simultaneously watched with them.

The nervous young woman reported, "The man the state police apprehended with the dead bodies is none other than Tobias St. John's chief of security, Nicholas Morris."

"Damn!" Tobias's gut tightened with frustration. He needed Nick, needed him to get Tabitha to safety. "Damn it…"

"What will you do now?" Jillian asked, her voice cracking with concern. "Can you put it off until he gets Morris out of jail?"

"I'm not sure he'll try," Tobias admitted, "or if he'd be successful."

"You think Morris killed someone?"

Tobias shook his head. "No. I know Edward did. He killed the guards who were supposed to bring you to him."

She gasped. "Oh, my God…"

The murders were on tape. But Tobias focused on the live feed as Edward summoned the car, then stalked out of the den. "He's going to run."

"But with the airfield…"

"He won't be able to leave."

"He'll come back when he finds out he can't get away. And Tabitha will definitely be in danger." She stepped closer to him and clutched his arm. "Let me help you. I can get onto the estate. I can get Tabitha into that room."

"It's too dangerous."

"But those men who were going to kill me, they're dead. They can't hurt me."

"Nick won't be there to protect you. And neither will I. I have to go to the meeting place." He glanced at his watch. "I have to get there before he does." *If he does…*

"He won't be at the house, then. I'll be safe," she said. "I can get Tabitha to safety."

Tobias shook his head. "I can't risk it." *I can't risk you.* He touched her face, cupping her cheek in his palm while he ran his thumb along her full bottom lip. She was so beautiful, but even more attractive than her beauty was her courage and strength. And he knew she was a survivor. Could he trust that she would survive this?

"Tobias." She said his name for the first time.

The first time anyone had called him by his name in a long while. He closed his eyes on a rush of emotion and relief. He hadn't entirely lost the man he'd once been. But if he let her do this, if he let her risk her life for him…

"She asked me for help," Jillian said. "That was days ago. And I didn't help her. I *need* to help her."

Because no one had helped the child she had once been? He suspected that she identified with his daughter. "If something happens to you…"

He would never forgive himself.

Chapter Twelve

Smoke darkened the sky as flames rose, lapping up metal and wood. Sparks shimmered as liquid and gas exploded. Shattered glass glistened like diamonds on the pavement of the airstrip. The planes, helicopter and hangar smoldered, blackened skeletons of metal.

"Stop the car," Edward directed the driver. He didn't want to get any closer to the fire. With the back window down, he could already feel the heat. And that was as close as he intended to get.

"Yes, sir," the chauffeur murmured, glancing fearfully into the rearview mirror before returning his attention to the burning hangar in front of them. "Do you think it was him?"

"Him?" Had people begun to suspect who was really behind the attacks on the city?

"The phantom?"

"Yeah. It was definitely *him*." The monster.

The beast. His brother had been called many things over the past two weeks, but never his own name. Along with the little girl, it was the last thing Tobias had yet to steal back from him.

Son of a bitch...

He'd taken everything Edward had wanted, including an escape route, which he needed right now. He didn't trust Morris to keep his mouth shut about how those men had died. His hand shook as he pulled the note from his pocket. *I have what you want....*

What he wanted had to include a plane or a helicopter—some way out of this damn city. Underneath that ominous message was the time and place for the exchange.

His mouth slid into a smirk. Soon he'd have nothing to exchange, though. He'd offered his own deal to the nanny. He would take her along with him when he left but only if she got rid of the kid.

She was too smart and too in love with him to fail him. Hell, the little girl was probably already dead.

As she had just a few nights before, Jillian stood outside the gates of Tobias St. John's estate. Before she'd left the underground tunnels, one of Tobias's men had brought her a change of clothes, so she was warm in jeans, a sweater and tennis shoes. They'd bought the things so she'd be comfortable as she'd traveled through the tunnels to a manhole outside the estate. But still, she shivered.

She stepped from the shadows into the glow of a streetlamp. She didn't have to worry about reporters camped across from the estate. A new barricade kept the media down the block, out of view of the house. No one could see her. For all intents and purposes, she was still missing. And if this went as badly as the muscles clenching in her stomach warned her, she could remain missing forever.

"Hello?"

No guards hovered behind the gates like they had a few nights ago. Hardly anyone walked near the cement fence inside the gates; she saw only a couple of hulking shadows near the house. Maybe the guards had figured out Edward wasn't Tobias. Maybe they'd realized he wouldn't be able to pay them. Or that he'd killed two of their colleagues. And so they'd quit. Or maybe he'd killed more than the two men whose bodies Morris had been caught disposing of.

"Hello?" she called out again.

Branches rustled. Loose asphalt crunched beneath feet as a dark shadow neared the gates. She swallowed hard, choking on her fear. She didn't have to do this. Even Tobias had told her that, had assured her that she didn't have to, that he really didn't want her to risk her life for his plan.

For his daughter.

Neither Tobias nor Tabitha meant anything to her. She barely knew them. But when she squeezed her eyes shut, she saw the little girl's face—her eyes wide with fear as she mouthed the words *Help me...*

"Ms. Drake?"

She opened her eyes to see a young guard. He peered through the gate, his brows arched with surprise at the sight of her. She smiled. "Yes, it's me."

He shook his head. "Everybody thinks you're dead."

Not yet. She swallowed a smart-ass comeback and held on to her friendly smile. "I'm very much alive. And I'd like to come inside."

"He's not here. He left a while ago."

"Mr. St. John?"

He hesitated slightly, as if he had begun to doubt the man's identity, and then nodded. "He's not here."

And that was the only reason she was. If the cameras hadn't caught him leaving, Tobias never would have let her out of the underground tunnels. "Let me wait for him inside."

The young guard shook his head.

"Come on," she cajoled him. "You know he wants to see me. If I leave, he won't be happy."

"I'm not sure he's coming back," he admitted.

"He's coming back," she assured him. But the only reason he'd return to the estate was because Tobias had blocked his every escape route.

"That's what she thinks, too."

"Tabitha?"

"Who? Oh, the little girl," he said. "No, the nanny. She's the one who's saying he's coming back. Lucky she didn't tell the police that, or they would have staked out the place."

"The police were here?" Had Morris told them the truth about the imposter? No, he wouldn't have risked Tabitha's life. They must have finally gotten suspicious on their own.

"Yeah. But they didn't have a search warrant, so I couldn't let them in. Why should I let you in, Ms. Drake?"

"Because you know he's going to be pissed if I just walk away." She turned from the gate and walked across the sidewalk. She slowed her steps, hoping he'd call her bluff. She couldn't just leave. What if Tabitha watched her from a window? What if she saw Jillian walk away again without trying to help her?

"Wait," the young man called out.

She expelled a quiet breath of relief before turning around. "Yes?"

Metal creaked and shuddered as the gates slid open. Her heart pounding hard, she walked through them and entered the estate. As the wrought-iron slid closed again, her breath burned in her lungs.

"You'll have to show yourself inside the house," the guard warned her. "Security is short-staffed right now. A lot of the guys are... gone." The young man's voice cracked with fear. "They're just...gone."

And she suspected that soon he would be, too, that he'd realized he was in as much danger as she'd just put herself in by walking through those gates.

This is crazy....

But she continued down the drive, to that imposing granite-and-glass structure. Either Edward or one of the guards had left in such a hurry that the front door swung open, blowing back and forth in the brisk breeze shaking the limbs of the overhanging trees.

She heard Tobias's voice in her head. "If anything feels off, get out."

The only thing about it that felt off was that it was too damn easy. It couldn't be this easy. Could it?

She stepped inside the house just as the lights flickered out. Tobias's men had blown the power plant. But the house must have a generator; the chandelier lit up again, casting an eerie glow onto the black marble foyer.

Dragging in a bracing breath, she headed up the stairwell toward the second story. Tabitha would be up there, but she wouldn't be alone. Jillian stepped from the landing into a wide hall lined with six-paneled doors.

Tobias had told her which one was his daughter's. Third door down. On the right or left? She couldn't remember, but she had to hurry—Edward was headed back right now. Her hand shaking with nerves, she reached for the black onyx knob of the door on the left. And Tobias's voice echoed inside her head with the instructions he'd given her before she'd left the underground. "Go straight to Tabitha's room. Get into the safe room with her and hit the alarm. Then no one can get in that room but me."

And her question rang in her mind. "What if something happens to you...?"

"Nothing will happen to me."

"He wants you dead," she'd reminded him. "He wouldn't have stolen your life if that wasn't what he wanted."

"No, he wants me to suffer." And hurting his little girl was the way to make Tobias suffer the most.

Thinking about it made Jillian shudder. She turned the knob and pushed open the door, but the room was empty of all but a made-up bed and dresser. She turned around just as a scream rang out. Her heart slammed against her ribs as she recognized the child's cry of terror.

She crossed the hall and flung open the door. Two figures struggled on the bed. Susan was pressing a pillow over Tabitha's face, but the child squirmed beneath her. Tabitha kicked out and flailed her arms, but the nanny was bigger. Stronger. The child's struggles already began to weaken as Jillian ran across the room.

She wrapped her arm around Susan's neck and jerked, trying to drag her off. The nanny screamed and thrashed her head, hitting Jillian's jaw. She stumbled back, but she took Susan with her. Her breath escaped her lungs as the nanny landed on top of her, jabbing her elbow in Jillian's ribs.

Jillian tightened her arm around the woman's neck, pressing on her throat. Susan clutched at the sleeve of Jillian's sweater, her nails tearing through the thick knit and cutting into Jillian's skin. She swung her head again, knocking her skull against Jillian's mouth.

Pain radiated from Jillian's lips and teeth all along her jaw. Blood trickled into her mouth, metallic and sweet, and ran down her chin. "You bitch," she murmured.

But she'd taken harder hits in her life. Some fake nanny wasn't going to get the best of her. Not when there was more than *her* life depending on her winning this fight.

Susan tugged free and scrambled up. But Jillian vaulted to her feet and grabbed her. The woman kicked her and swung her fist, but her blow glanced off Jillian's shoulder.

Jillian struck back, her fist connecting with the blonde's jaw. The woman's eyes rolled back, and she dropped to the floor. Jillian ignored the stinging in her knuckles. Her pulse racing with adrenaline and fear, she turned back to the bed, which was empty. Then blue eyes peered just above the mattress.

"Are you okay, honey?" she asked the little girl.

Tabitha nodded. "Is—is she dead?" she asked, her voice as raspy as her father's.

Jillian scrambled around the bed and held out her arms for the child. "She's not dead. But you're safe." For now.

Tabitha shook her head even as she crawled onto Jillian's lap. "It's not safe. Not here."

Jillian rested her chin onto the top of the dark curls and sighed. The little girl was right. It wasn't safe in this house—not even in that special room, especially if the only one who could free them was meeting with a killer. She needed to get her out of there, off the damn estate entirely.

The nanny lay on the floor, unconscious. The guards might have all left by now. No one would stop her from just walking through the gates.

"We're going to leave," she agreed with the child. "Let's go…"

"You're hurt," Tabitha said, her fingertip gently touching Jillian's lip.

"It'll be fine," she assured the little girl. "We have to get out of here."

She lifted up the little girl, balancing her slight weight on her hip. Tabitha's arms wrapped tightly around her. Jillian's heart pounded as she hurried out the bedroom door and down the hall toward the stairs.

The lights flickered again. The generator was losing power. Had Tobias's men tampered with it? Had that been part of their mission?

Jillian realized she didn't know everything about the plan, only her part in it. To get Tabitha to safety. But as she started down the stairs, headlights penetrated the leaded glass of the front door and glinted off the dimming chandelier.

"It's him," Tabitha said, her voice quavering

with fear. "He's back." She locked her arms around Jillian's neck in a stranglehold.

"It could be your dad."

"My dad?" the child asked, her eyes wide with hope. "He's alive?"

"Yes," Jillian replied, hoping she told the child the truth. "This whole time he's been gone, he's been working on a plan to rescue you. He's coming home."

"But—but what if that's not Daddy?" Tabitha asked.

Then she would have failed her part of the plan. Goose bumps lifted on Jillian's skin, and she turned on the stairs, running back up them. "I won't let him hurt you," she promised the child. "I won't…"

Jostling the little girl in her arms, she ran down the hall toward Tabitha's bedroom. The nanny still lay on the floor, unmoving. Jillian slammed the door with her back, then fumbled for a lock.

"He took it off," the little girl said, wriggling out of Jillian's arms. "We can hide under the bed…"

"No. Your daddy made a better hiding spot for you," she said. First, using her hip, she shoved a dresser in front of the door. Then she caught the little girl's hand and tugged her toward the closet. She pulled the doors open, then shoved the clothes aside.

"He wants us to hide in here?" Tabitha asked doubtfully. "He'll find us in here...."

"No, there's a secret room." But as she pounded against the wall, she couldn't find the switch that would slide the panel open. Footfalls on the stairs echoed her pounding, and then grew louder as he neared the door.

"Daddy's home," the man called out. "Come here." The knob rattled as he turned it.

A cry slipped through Tabitha's lips. "It's not Daddy...."

The tingling on Jillian's nape told her the same thing. She pounded hard, striking her palms against the wood until finally something clicked. It slid open just as the lights flickered off.

"Get inside," she said, hoping the power outage wouldn't render the safe room useless. But it must have had its own generator, for a light illuminated the small space. Tobias might not have had time to stock the tiny kitchenette, but he'd furnished the room with a bed, a couch and television.

As the door to the hall opened and struck

against the dresser, Jillian urged the frightened little girl inside the secret room. The dresser teetered, then fell over with a crash of splintering wood and shattering glass. Jillian had just stepped inside the room when a big hand closed around her arm, jerking her back.

"What the hell is this?" he asked.

It was too late for her. He was too strong for her to fight like she had the nanny. But she could keep her promise to Tabitha. Fumbling for the control panel on the wall just inside the room, she pushed the button that activated the door. Then she summoned all her strength and shoved her shoulder into Edward St. John's chest. He stumbled backward, dragging her with him.

Tabitha screamed, her voice pitched high with fear. But the panel slid closed, locking the little girl safely inside where her deranged uncle couldn't hurt her.

"Open the door!" he yelled at Jillian, shaking her arm so roughly her shoulder popped.

"No."

Despite the utter blackness in the closet, his

fist still connected with her face, knocking her against the panel. "Open it!"

Tears of pain stung her eyes, but she blinked them back. She hadn't been much older than Tabitha when she'd learned she couldn't betray any weakness to a bully and a coward. And that was all Edward St. John was.

"I can't open it," she replied in all honesty. Once the inside lock was engaged, a code had to be entered into a hidden control panel in order to deactivate the safe room door. "Only Tobias can."

He sucked in a breath. "He told you?"

Her cheek throbbing, she managed a nod. "I know you're an imposter."

"So he's coming here?" he asked, twisting her arm as he dragged her from the closet.

"Not until after his meeting with you," she said, trying to wrestle free of his punishing grip. "He's coming here after the exchange."

"Exchange?" Edward snorted. "You mean my murder? That's what he's planning—to lure me to one of those warehouses and blow me up."

A gasp of shock and realization slipped out of her swollen lips. Was part of Tobias's plan...*murder?*

"You didn't realize that when you signed on to help him?" he asked, astutely reading her even in the dark. "You didn't understand that you were going to become an accomplice to murder?"

She shook her head. "No," she denied, despite her doubts. "He's not going to kill you."

"You are so naive," the madman scoffed. "You think he's going to let me live after I stole his life from him? You don't think he's going to take mine out of vengeance?"

"No."

"Then you don't know him at all, Miss Drake."

"You don't know him," she pointed out. "He doesn't care about vengeance. He cares about Tabitha. He intends to pay you a ransom for his daughter. He has money, stock…"

"But yet he sent you here to hide her away from me. How am I to bring my part of the exchange to the meeting now?"

"Use me," she offered. "Bring me with you."

He laughed. "He only agreed to this exchange because I have what matters most to him. His daughter. You think he cares about you?"

No. But again, she wouldn't reveal her weakness to this bully. "Yes."

"If he cares so damn much, why would he send you here? Why would he risk your life for hers? He doesn't give a damn about you, Miss Drake."

She flinched, her heart aching with a pain more intense than the result of any of the punches she'd taken. She had already fallen for Tobias.

"No," Edward continued. "It's time I cut my losses and leave."

"The police are looking for you," she reminded him. "You're not going to be able to take a commercial flight. And there are too many barricades for you to just drive out of the city."

"With what I have planned, they won't be looking for me."

"He'll be looking for you," she said. "Tobias is coming back."

"He'll be too late," he said. "He won't be able to save his daughter. Or you."

TOBIAS HAD EXPECTED a battle. Hell, he had anticipated a war. So he was almost disappointed to simply walk through the open gates. The lone guard left on duty merely nodded at him. "Mr. St. John…"

He had ditched the mask and contacts. Jillian and Tabitha should be in the safe room by now, out of the cruel grasp of Edward St. John. So it didn't matter anymore who saw him.

"Where is *he?*" he asked.

"Who?" the guard replied. "Nick Morris?"

"No. The man who looks like me—" Tobias lifted the flashlight beam to his face "—the one who took over the house a couple of weeks ago."

The guard's brow furrowed. "What man? That was a different man?"

"My twin." He swallowed down bile with the admission. "Where is he?" Tobias repeated his question.

The guy blinked, then stammered, "You— he—just left in the car. I didn't know why… with the power down across the city. I thought that was why you came back…because you couldn't get anywhere."

Edward would be able to get to their meeting place, though, since Tobias had moved the barricades between the estate and their warehouse assignation.

"Did he leave alone?" Tobias asked. Had Jillian gotten her and Tabitha to the safe room before Edward had returned?

The man shrugged. "I don't know. I didn't see him leave the house, and the windows of the limo are tinted. I couldn't see inside...."

Tobias glanced at the house. All of its windows were dark now, too—the generator shut down to buy Jillian time to make it to Tabitha's room. He had only one way of learning if this part of his plan had been successful.

He had only to go home...

His breath catching in his lungs, he headed toward the front door. Soon he would hold his baby in his arms again, to feel her close to his heart. But she wasn't the only female he wanted to hold again. He needed to see Jillian, too, to convince himself that she was safe, that he hadn't risked her life.

But as he reached for the knob, the house shuddered and rumbled. Then it exploded.

Chapter Thirteen

The flames rose like tongues lapping at the night sky. Edward trembled with excitement as he watched through the back window of the limo as it circled around the block. *It was perfect...absolutely perfect.*

"I hope he burns to death," he said. And once his twin's body was recovered, no one would be looking for him. Edward would be free to leave just as he'd arrived—unfortunately, with nothing.

But at least Tobias had nothing, too. Not his empire, his daughter or even his life...

"You should have been in that fire, too," Edward told the woman sitting on the back-seat beside him. "I should have let you burn alive in the house...just like his daughter did."

Jillian could barely restrain her sobs. With

blood crusted on her swollen lip and her hair disheveled, she didn't look as beautiful as she always did on television. But she drew his attention and his attraction. Edward had never met a woman as strong as Jillian Drake, one who fought instead of using tears to try to soften a man. She was nearly as full of fire as Tobias's mansion. Maybe he wasn't leaving with nothing, after all.

"You better hope he's dead," the reporter warned him. "Because if you hurt Tabitha and he survived, he'll make you suffer."

He laughed uneasily. Had Tobias been close enough when Edward had triggered the explosion? Since the driveway wound away from the gates, he hadn't been able to see if his twin had made it inside before he'd detonated the bomb. His brother wasn't the only one with explosives expertise learned as a Special Forces marine. One of the mercenaries had known enough to wire the bomb inside the house for when Tobias made his final move.

Through the open window, the soft wail of sirens signaled the approach of the authorities. Soon they would find Tobias's body, but Edward wouldn't be able to wait around to watch them drag the charred remains from the house. He had to hide now, like his brother had been forced to hide. Urgency quickening his pulse, he directed the chauffeur. "Drive."

"Where do you want me to go, Mr. St. John?" the young man asked, anxiety in his voice and in the gaze that met Edward's in the rearview mirror.

Edward paused, his head pounding now. He hadn't thought beyond this moment, beyond his brother's pain.

"The warehouse," the woman suggested, "where you were supposed to meet Tobias."

"You think I'm stupid?" he asked, clenching her shoulder in his fist to shake her, as anger heated his blood. "You think I'm going to blindly walk into the trap he set for me?"

"He's here," she pointed out. "And it's there—the ransom he promised you. I saw it. The money. The jewelry."

The future. Edward could see it, too. But dare he trust her? Dare he trust Tobias?

"He wouldn't lie to you—not when he thought it could save Tabitha's life." Her voice quavering with the tears she had yet to shed, she added, "In exchange for his daughter, he would give you *anything* you wanted."

Edward chuckled at his brother's weakness.

Maybe their mother had done him a favor by selling him. She'd raised his brother to be weak.

"Even you?" he asked the redhead. "Do you think he intended for you to be part of the ransom?"

He wanted her to see that his brother was no hero. He was no better than Edward. Their mother had had no reason to keep Tobias and discard him.

"You can't hurt him anymore," she said as she gestured toward the smoke billowing over the cement wall surrounding the estate.

The flames had already died down; hopefully the blast had been enough to kill him since the fire might not have burned long enough to do the job.

Her voice soft and resigned, she murmured, "He's gone."

Disappointment flashed through Edward. Maybe he'd killed Tobias too quickly. Too impersonally. He'd never actually had the chance to meet his brother face-to-face, to see the life ebb from his eyes as Edward took it all away from him. "Yeah, he's gone...."

"You have to leave now," she advised him. "Before someone sees you here, before someone realizes that there were two of you."

Until he'd finally tracked down his birth mother, he hadn't realized there was someone else out there, someone with his face, his voice…his life. The life he should have been living. Instead of all those years he'd spent behind bars, paying for crimes he wouldn't have had to commit if things had gone differently for him. If he'd had someone who'd actually given a damn about him…

His grip tightened on her arm. He had someone now. And he wasn't going to let her go…not until he knew for certain if the ransom existed.

"Okay," he consented, and gave the address of the warehouse to the driver. "Let's go see what I inherited from my dearly departed brother.…"

WATER RAINED DOWN from the sprinklers, dousing the flames as well as his hair and his clothes. But the wood was still hot and brittle beneath Tobias's feet as he ran up the stairs. The fire had done more damage than the blast. The bomb hadn't been powerful enough to destroy the reinforced structure of the house.

But how much damage had the fire done…?

Smoke filled the house, adding to the complete darkness, so he stumbled down the hall. The walls were hot beneath his touch as he felt around for the door to his little girl's room. It stood open, and faint light streaked through the bars on the broken window. The moonlight fell across a body on the floor beside what was left of his daughter's bed. Before the water had doused them, flames had burned the clothes and charred the flesh. He covered his nose and mouth at the gruesome scent of it, as horror filled him.

Too big to be a child, it had to be…

"Not Jillian." Tears stung his eyes from more than the smoke. "Please God…"

He stepped closer, his legs shaking slightly as the weakened floor trembled beneath his weight. Until someone could check dental records, there would be no way to identify the body. No way to know if Jillian had made the ultimate sacrifice for him and his daughter…

Tabitha…

Had Jillian managed to get her inside the safe room? His heart pounding hard, he headed toward the closet. The charred floorboards protested his weight. No matter how strong the structure of that panic room, it required the support of the rest of the house or it would drop into the basement, proving more tomb than refuge.

He fumbled inside what was left of the closet. His daughter's clothes were tattered rags hanging from blackened metal hangers. Some of the metal of the sliding door had burned off. Blackened, the control panel was indiscernible in the dark. He reached inside his pocket for the remote system for the room; the switch looked no different from a car's keyless entry control. It was what he'd held up in the parking garage that morning, what had saved him and Jillian from getting shot.

Hopefully it had saved her again. He clicked a button, and the scorched panel creaked open, the wood cracking and splintering against the steel of the panic room door.

A blast of fresh air washed over him, relieving some of that tension in his gut. The explosion hadn't compromised the room, or the generator that powered the light. His little girl sat on the bed in the corner, her arms wrapped around her legs, her head on her knees as she sobbed.

His gut clenched again with pain. Tabitha was terrified. And she was alone. Jillian hadn't made it inside with her, but she had kept her promise to keep his daughter safe.

His throat thick with emotion, he could only whisper her name. "Tabitha…"

A cry slipped from the little girl's lips, and she trembled in fear.

"Honey, it's me," he assured his daughter as he dropped to his knees just inside the doorway. For the first time ever, Tobias wanted to make himself smaller and less threatening. "Sweetheart, I swear that it's really *me*. It's your daddy."

She lifted her head just an inch or so, just so she could peer over her knees at him. Her blue eyes narrowed with suspicion and hatred as she met his gaze. Her soft voice sharp with a bitterness he'd never heard from her before, she asked, "Really?"

Pain clutched at his chest—pain at having his own child look at him like that, with fear and hatred. He nodded and lifted his little finger. "Pinkie swear—it's me."

Her body tensed as she studied him silently. The suspicion remained; she didn't trust him. And he couldn't blame her. He'd vowed to be a better parent than his mother had been; he'd vowed to protect her. But he'd failed her.

"Oh, baby…" His voice broke, and he uttered a ragged sigh of defeat. "I'm so sorry…."

Tabitha jumped up from the bed and threw herself at him. "Daddy! My daddy!"

He wrapped his arms tight around her fragile little body. "Tabitha, my sweetheart…."

The little girl sobbed, her tears dampening his neck as she burrowed close. "Daddy, you're here. You're really here!"

"I'm really here," he assured her. "And I won't leave you again. I promise." The floor creaked, and the steel-walled room shuddered. "I won't leave you, but we have to get out of here." The lights dimmed and the air filter clanked and clattered. "Now."

He backed out the open panel of the safe room and headed across the floor toward the door to the hall, careful to keep his shoulder between Tabitha's head and the body lying on the floor beside the bed. But she glimpsed it, her breath catching. "She's dead…."

"Yeah…" He couldn't lie to her. As well as always protecting her, he'd promised himself that he would never lie to her.

"I—I thought *you* were dead," Tabitha murmured with a sniffle. She must have believed that was the only reason he would have stayed away from her. "But Jilly told me you were alive, that you were coming…"

Before giving up her own life, she had sought to comfort his daughter.

"I tried to get home sooner," Tobias said as he hurried back down the creaking stairs, water trickling from the sprinklers onto them. "But I couldn't…"

Tabitha ducked her head beneath his chin and trembled again, but not because the cold water chilled her. "Because of the bad man. He's gone?"

"He's gone." For now. And with the wail of sirens growing louder, he doubted Edward would be returning anytime soon.

"Where is she?"

"Who?" Tobias asked as he hesitated just outside the front door. If he stepped out there, if the police saw him…

But the gates were closed again; all the

guards were gone. It would take some time for the authorities to gain access.

"Jilly," Tabitha said, cupping his cheek in her small hand so that he turned back to her. "The lady from TV. Where is she?"

Maybe it was the smoke that stung his eyes; maybe it was an emotion he couldn't give in to yet. But more than regret filled him when he thought of Jillian Drake. Tobias had never met a more selfless woman. She had thought nothing of her own safety, her own life, when she'd rescued his daughter.

Damn her...

Damn her for putting herself in danger. He squeezed his eyes shut. "I—I don't know," he answered honestly. Maybe it wasn't her body. God, he hoped it wasn't her body....

"She helped me," Tabitha said. "I asked her to help me days ago. And I didn't think she heard me. But she came back. She helped me."

"I know." If not for Jillian Drake, his daughter would have certainly been dead.

Tabitha shook her head, and tears streamed down her face. "Susan had a pillow on my face. I—I couldn't breathe. And—and I couldn't fight her anymore..."

Tobias shuddered at the horror his baby had endured. "Oh, sweetheart…"

"But Jilly saved me," she said, her voice querulous. "She—she got hurt. Nanny Susan made her bleed."

Tobias's breath caught at the thought of what both females he'd cared about had suffered. "Oh, my God…"

"But she knocked out the nanny," Tabitha said with grim satisfaction. "That's who—who's up in my room…on the floor by my bed."

The nanny. Tobias had forgotten all about her, and he'd never realized the threat she'd posed. She'd almost killed his daughter. If not for Jillian, she would have.

The reporter hadn't been kidding when she'd claimed to be a survivor. He expelled a ragged breath of relief. Maybe she hadn't given up everything for him. "So Jillian got out…before the explosion?"

Her eyes wide and bright with tears, Tabitha nodded. "*He* took her. The bad man has Jilly."

Jillian might have stood a better chance of surviving the explosion and subsequent fire. "No…"

"Do you know where he took her?" Tabitha asked him. "Do you know where she is?"

The man had nothing now—no means of escape but for the ransom Tobias had promised him. "I think so."

She wriggled down from his arms. "Then you have to go. You have to save her."

Tobias hesitated at leaving his baby girl standing alone on the driveway in front of their fire-damaged home. "I'm sorry, sweetheart. I know I just promised you that I wouldn't leave you again. But you won't be alone long. There are firemen and policemen coming. They'll protect you. And Mr. Morris will be here soon."

He'd had the security footage delivered to the police department so that his friend would be cleared of murder charges. Of course his friend would probably still be charged as an accessory after the fact, but the lawyer to whom Tobias had also sent the footage should be able to get him out on bail.

Tabitha stepped forward and reached out, but instead of closing her arms around him again, she shoved at him. "Go, Daddy, go save Jilly," she urgently advised him.

He nodded, overwhelmed by the maturity

and generosity of the five-year-old. But he couldn't make her a promise that he might already be too late to keep.

Jillian had protected Tabitha from Edward, but the man was smart enough to know that she mattered to Tobias, too. And he only went after what mattered most to Tobias.

Until he'd found that body lying on the floor of his daughter's bedroom, he hadn't realized exactly how much the reporter mattered to him. He loved Jillian Drake. And now he was about to lose her.

Chapter Fourteen

As the car neared the warehouse, Jillian's heart beat harder and faster. She'd bought herself some time. But not enough.

"So tell me about yourself," she said. The men she had known that were arrogant and self-absorbed like Edward St. John—her dad and her ex—could spend hours talking about themselves. "I don't even know your name…."

"You know, Miss Drake, because he told you," he said, his voice sharp with impatience. "Tobias told you everything about me."

"He doesn't know much," she reminded him. "He didn't even know you existed."

"He's lying," Edward insisted.

She shook her head. "You know he had no idea, that he was shocked…"

He chuckled. "Shocked that someone out-smarted and outmaneuvered him."

She shivered, more at the evilness in the man's face than his words. How could he look so much like Tobias, share the same handsome features, his strong jaw and arresting blue eyes, but be so ugly inside?

"He had to have known about me," Edward insisted. "Because she kept him. She raised him."

"She never told him the truth. I don't think he had it easy, staying with her. You might have been luckier that she gave you up."

"She sold me," Edward bitterly corrected her, "exchanging me for drug money. Then I was sold again—to a woman who was too old to have a baby of her own and too screwed up to adopt. Then when she got desperate for drugs, she sold me, too. I was passed around because no one wanted to keep me."

"I'm sorry," she said. "But it doesn't excuse what you've done. None of this is Tobias's fault. And it's certainly not Tabitha's. She's just a child."

"Was," he said with that evil smirk. "She couldn't have survived the blast."

Just how secure had Tobias made that panic

room? She hoped safe enough to protect his daughter. "She's your niece. Doesn't that matter to you? Don't you care?"

He shook his head. "I learned young that everyone's expendable. That's something my brother and I have in common. I warned you, Miss Drake, that he was just using you. You should have listened to me."

She lifted her chin, refusing to let him get to her. After three years of studying him, after making love with him, she knew Tobias better than this man did. "I talked him into letting me help. I had to convince him."

"He's good," Edward said with some respect. "He's quite the manipulator."

"He didn't manipulate me," Jillian insisted. She'd been manipulated before—into believing things were her fault that weren't, into thinking she deserved things that she hadn't. "I wanted to help."

But had she helped? Or were both Tobias and his daughter dead? Would she have been smarter to have gone right to the police instead of the estate? But she couldn't have trusted them.

Emotion choked her, but she fought back the tears. She couldn't give in to them now, not when her own life was in danger. She peered through the windows as the limo pulled into the empty lot of a dark warehouse.

"This better not be a trick," Edward warned her. He reached beneath his dark suit jacket and pulled a gun from the waistband of his pants.

He could have used it earlier, could have shot both her and Tabitha. Maybe, despite his claims to not care, he hadn't quite been able to harm the child himself. Instead, he'd ordered the nanny to do his dirty work.

"You don't need the gun," she assured him, hoping he'd leave it in the car. "You saw him… back at the estate. He's not here."

The driver opened the back door for them, his eyes widening with fear as he spotted the weapon. Unlike some of the guards, he obviously wasn't a mercenary.

"You know he wasn't working alone these past couple of weeks," Edward reminded her. "He couldn't have managed all that destruction by himself. Someone even died helping him. That should have been another warning for you to stay away from him."

"I was after a story," she defended herself.

"Too bad you won't live to report it," Edward said as he grabbed her hair and dragged her out of the car with him.

"Help me," she implored the driver. But the man turned his back to her and slid through the open driver's door. "He's not Tobias St. John. He's an imposter."

Edward slapped her, knocking her to the pavement. Asphalt bit into her palms as she caught herself. Then his hand was in her hair again, jerking her to her feet.

Tears stung her eyes, but she blinked them back, ignoring the pain. Tobias hadn't confided his entire plan to her, but he wouldn't have agreed to meet this madman alone. Would he have? Shouldn't there be someone inside the warehouse, as Edward feared? Someone willing to help her since the driver was not?

Edward shoved her forward, toward the open door of the warehouse. Then he stopped and listened before pushing her across the threshold first.

"Hello?" she called out, making sure that because of the complete darkness, no one would mistake her for Edward.

She should have gotten more of Tobias's plan

out of him. But he hadn't trusted her, even after she'd offered to help. Was his brother right? Had he only been using her?

"Is anyone here?" she asked, her voice cracking with despair.

Edward's hand clenched in her hair, but he said nothing, just jerked her forward.

Jillian stumbled into a crate, and pain radiated up her leg. "You should have brought a flashlight," she murmured, "instead of a gun."

"What is all this?" he asked in a raspy whisper eerily reminiscent of Tobias's voice.

"It's the ransom," she said, running her hands over the top of the crate nearest her. Something dropped from the corner, metal clanging against cement. A crowbar?

She reached inside the crate and pulled out a handful of jewelry. The stones glinted in the light of the limo's headlamps shining through the open door. "Tobias isn't like you," she said. "He keeps his word."

Edward pulled his hand from her hair and reached for the jewelry. Purposely, she missed his palm and dropped the necklaces onto the ground.

"Sorry…" As she crouched to pick up the

jewelry, her foot bumped against the crowbar. She reached behind her, grabbed it up and swung it widely, knocking it against his face and shoulder.

Curses echoed off the metal walls of the old warehouse. "You bitch!"

Her heart pounding hard against her ribs, she darted out of his reach to the other side of the crate. A shot rang out, splintering wood and glancing off metal. She ran through the maze of crates, wooden barrels and pallets that had been piled high in the warehouse. Knocking against the obstacles in the dark, she telegraphed her every move to the man who chased after her.

"I'm going to find you," he shouted, heedless now of anyone overhearing him. "Then I'm going to kill you."

She shuddered with fear, knowing that he could carry out his threat. In some ways he was like his brother—true to his word and single-minded.

"I'll find you!" Edward promised her. He kicked aside barrels. Wood splintered as he threw plywood and pallets.

Crouched behind a row of crates, Jillian held her breath. She had to hide, even though her legs ached to run. So she shrank lower, so close to the ground that the cold cement chilled her skin to the bone.

Something crackled, then buzzed, and the fluorescent bulbs beamed on overhead, bathing the entire warehouse in bright light.

He laughed. "It's no use hiding from me now."

She trembled with fear. He was right. She needed to run, or stand and fight. Her grip tightened on the crowbar. The light could help her, too. This time when she hit him, she'd hit him hard enough…

But before she could rise from her crouch, a shadow fell across her. Edward reached down, grabbed her hair and dragged her to her feet. Then he pressed the cold barrel of his gun against her temple. "Drop that damn crowbar or I'll blow your brains out right here."

She dropped her weapon, which clanged against the cement floor. It was too late for her to fight now. One twitch of his finger against that trigger, and she was dead. Like Tobias and Tabitha?

"What are you going to do?" she asked him. If he intended to *hurt* her, she might rather that he just shot her now.

"I'm going to get the driver—we'll load the limo with this stuff," he said. "I just can't figure out whether I should kill you before or after…."

"Hear that?" she asked, catching the sound of a motor as the limo pulled out of the lot. "He left you here."

"No!" he shouted, making her flinch in pain as he dragged her closer to the open door. "He wouldn't dare. He wouldn't defy me."

The taillights disappeared as the car turned onto another street. "He's gone."

"Damn it…" he murmured, loosening his grip on her enough that she pulled away.

Jillian barely restrained the urge to laugh at his frustration, but she couldn't resist pointing out, "Now that everyone knows you're not Tobias, you've lost your power. Hell, it was never really yours, anyway. It was his."

Edward lifted the gun, pointing the barrel between her eyes. "I still have power over you. Your life is literally in my hands."

AND BECAUSE OF THAT, because Edward held a gun to the head of the woman Tobias loved, his brother still had power over him. He cursed himself now for not carrying the gun Morris had brought him two weeks ago when he'd first returned to River City.

"Just shoot him…"

"I can't get close enough," he'd explained. But the truth was he hadn't wanted to kill; he'd done enough of that in the Special Forces. He hadn't wanted anyone to die.

Until now.

"Then let me kill him," Morris had offered.

"No, it's too risky. You kill him, and those mercenaries he hired will kill you." Tobias hadn't wanted to lose his longtime friend or Tabitha's protector. But in the end, it hadn't been Morris who had protected his daughter.

Jillian had.

He wanted to protect her now. Despite the bright lights overhead, he managed to keep to the shadows where he'd spent the past two weeks. He slunk around the crates, circling behind them.

"You can try to talk me into sparing your life," Edward suggested, his deep voice full of innuendo. "Even now, you're a beautiful woman…"

Tobias had known other beautiful women—his mother, his ex—who would have accepted such an offer, who would have done anything to get what they wanted. His ex had gotten pregnant to trap him into marriage. She'd threatened to terminate the pregnancy if he hadn't given her what she'd wanted. She hadn't wanted him or his daughter. Like Edward, she'd only wanted money.

Instead of accepting his offer, Jillian spat in Edward's face. With her spittle dripping from his chin, the man lifted the gun again.

His heart pounding, Tobias hurled the cover of a crate, knocking Edward to the ground. The gun dropped from his grasp and skittered across the floor, metal scraping against cement. Jillian stumbled back; then she gazed up at him, her green eyes wide with shock.

"I thought you were dead," Edward said with a groan as he rolled over and eased up onto his knees.

"You thought wrong," Tobias corrected him, "about everything."

Edward shook his head. "Oh, I don't think so. You wouldn't be here if your little girl needed you."

"She doesn't need me."

Jillian gasped. "Oh, no. She's not…"

"She's fine," Tobias assured her. "She told me to save Jilly."

Tears glistened in those green eyes…for just a moment before she blinked them back.

"You should have stayed with your daughter," Edward advised him as he lurched to his feet. "Because you're not leaving here alive." He reached for Jillian, catching her hair in his hand. "And neither is she."

Tobias vaulted over the crate so that he finally stood face-to-face with the man who'd stolen his life. "You're going to let her go."

Edward laughed. "Don't you get it yet? What else do I have to take away from you for you to understand that you have no power over me?"

Not Jillian. But if he said that, his brother was certain to kill her—right in front of Tobias's eyes.

"Look around you," he urged the madman. "This is all that's left of what I had. And I'm giving it to you. All you have to do is take it and leave. There's a truck in the back. We'll get it loaded for you. And I'll make sure no one stops you. You can drive far away from River City."

"I'll take the stuff," Edward agreed. "But

I'm taking her, too." He jerked Jillian by her thick red hair, and the tears glistening in her eyes spilled onto her face. But she didn't cry out.

"You're going to let Jillian go," Tobias repeated calmly. "Because this…war of ours… doesn't concern her. This is about you and me."

"There is no you and me." His twin snorted with derision. "There hasn't been since the womb."

"I didn't know about you," Tobias insisted. "She never told me."

"She forgot all about me?"

"Hell, most of the time she forgot about me," Tobias said. "She was so strung out. So messed up…"

"Then why did she pick you to keep and me to sell?" Edward asked, his deep voice full of torment.

Tobias shrugged. "I don't know. She didn't care about either of us."

"But if she'd kept me, I would have your life now. All of this would have been mine."

"No," Jillian answered for him. "You would have had to work for it. You would have had to have brains and ambition—not just greed."

Edward jerked her hair so hard that her neck cracked. A little harder and it could break. Tobias didn't think, he just reacted, slamming his fist into a face so similar to his own.

"You son of a bitch!" Edward cursed as blood spurted from his nose. But he released her. Jillian fell to her knees, barely crawling out of the way before Edward lunged at Tobias.

His fist connected with Tobias's jaw, knocking him back. But Edward didn't fight fair; he kicked and bit. And as they fell to the ground, he wrapped his hands around Tobias's throat, squeezing off his air.

Tobias pounded his fists into the other man's ribs and back, but Edward's grip didn't ease. His face—that damned identical face—swam before Tobias's blurring vision as he fought…to hang on to consciousness.

He couldn't pass out. He had to fight, had to protect Jillian. Or Edward would kill her, too.

THE TWO MEN—so identical in appearance—grappled, knocking aside barrels and wooden crates and pallets as they rolled around the cement floor of the crowded warehouse. Fists flew and the men grunted as their blows connected.

Jillian crawled forward, feeling across the cement for the crowbar or the gun—anything she could use as a weapon. She had to find something to help Tobias. The fluorescent lights glinted off metal, partially hidden beneath the corner of a crate. She eased her fingers between the pallet and the wooden box, clawing at the weapon until it slid from its hiding place.

Her breath caught as she stared down at the gun. Could she…use it? She knew how. Ironically her father had been the one to teach her to shoot. He'd been too arrogant to consider that he might have been the one she'd want to shoot.

But he had locked up his guns. She'd used them only on the firing range. She could shoot—at targets. But could she point the barrel at a human?

Grunts echoed off the metal walls and ceiling of the warehouse. She heard a groan, and a gasp for breath, as she turned back to the men. She wasn't the only one who'd changed clothes before leaving the underground tunnels. So that he could get past security at his own estate, Tobias had dressed in a dark suit identical to the one they'd seen Edward wearing on the security footage. The black silk shirt lay open at the collar. Both men were disheveled, from rolling around on the cement, and bruised from the fists they threw at each other. Blood trickled from the nose of one of them and the lip of the other. Their dark hair, the same blue-black shade, hung nearly to their broad shoulders.

Their hands, so big and strong, wrapped tightly around each other's throat, squeezing the life from each other. One of those men was Tobias. What if he was the one who gave up first, who died at the hands of his twin?

She had to do something, had to help him. Her hands trembled on the gun, though. What if she shot the wrong man? She would be killing her lover and Tabitha's father….

A rough chuckle, punctuated with grunts and pants, echoed in the warehouse. "Look, she can't tell us apart…."

Jillian took aim and pulled the trigger.

Chapter Fifteen

"Oh, my God…" Jillian murmured, her eyes wide with horror as she stared at the man lying on the ground. Blood oozed from his chest and pooled on the cement floor. "Oh, my…"

Tobias gently eased the gun from her shaking hands. Then he pulled her into his arms and clutched her close to his madly pounding heart. "Are you all right? Are you all right?"

"Yes," she assured him, but she trembled as she clung to him. "Is he…is he dead?"

A groan from his twin answered her. Edward clutched his hand against the right side of his chest; the bullet had missed his heart, but might have struck a lung.

"Not yet," Tobias said. Sirens, in the distance, grew louder as emergency vehicles finally approached. To make certain he'd have backup, Tobias had called them from his cell before entering the warehouse. With help coming, Edward would probably be okay. Tobias breathed a slight sigh of relief, for Jillian only. He didn't want her to have to live with killing a man; it wasn't something a person ever really got over. Unless that person was like his twin, more animal than human. "How did you know which one of us…?"

Her fingers, shaking still, slid over his naked face. "He couldn't resist taunting you, gloating…."

No, he couldn't—because Edward hated him that much. Tobias had pissed off people over the years—during his stint in the service and in business—but he'd never had someone despise him just for being born.

"The minute he did that," she continued, "I knew which one of you he was…."

"It was stupid of him to give himself away like that," Tobias murmured with a glance at his bleeding twin. But then Edward was so arrogant he was ignorant; he probably hadn't believed she'd actually shoot.

"If you hadn't pulled that trigger, you and I would probably both be dead now," he said.

She shuddered and glanced again at the man lying on the ground. But Tobias tipped up her chin, and his heart clenched at the sight of the vivid bruises on her otherwise alabaster skin. This battle between him and his brother hadn't been her fight, yet she'd fought—for his daughter and for him.

"Thank you…" The words were inadequate to express his gratitude.

"Tabitha's really okay?" she asked. "I don't think you'd leave her if she was hurt. But I need to know that she's all right. When the house exploded, I thought you'd both been killed."

"She told me to save Jilly," he reminded her.

Those tears glistened in her eyes again as she nodded. "When you said that, I knew you'd talked to her. That's what she calls me…."

"You saved my little girl," he said, and damned if tears didn't sting his own eyes. But he blinked back the threat of moisture; he hadn't cried since he'd been about Tabitha's age. Because, like Jillian, he'd had no one to cry to.

"And you just saved me now," he said. Thanking her was inadequate.

So he kissed her, gently brushing his lips across her swollen ones. It was all he had time for as the warehouse exploded with lights and to the commotion of the police shouting, "Freeze!"

It was over, or so he thought until a SWAT officer knocked him to the ground and handcuffed his wrists behind his back. "You're under arrest…"

The words rang in his ears with the realization that it wasn't over; it may not be over for a long while. He hadn't just lost everything he'd spent his life building; he might have lost his freedom, too.

He had nothing to offer Jillian Drake. He had no right to say the words burning in his throat. *I love you…*

And so he restrained himself from making the declaration. He didn't dare to even look at her as the police led him away. He wouldn't make her a promise he might not be able to keep.

FLASHBULBS AND LIGHTS blinded Jillian as she stepped out of the police department, after what had seemed like hours of answering questions as state troopers had written up her statement. Like her, the state police department had lost faith in the local authorities. The media surrounded her, pushing mikes into her face. She squinted and lifted her hand, not to block their shots but to shield her sensitive eyes. Exhaustion had already begun to blur her vision; she had no fight left in her now.

"Jillian, can you tell us what you know about Tobias St. John's involvement in the siege on the city?"

She could, but she'd made a promise. So she summoned enough energy to push her way through the crowd, pulling away from the hands that clutched at her. But then someone threw her arms around Jillian's neck.

"Thank God, you're alive," Vicky said, her voice cracking on a sob. "I thought...I thought..."

"The whole damn city thought the same thing," Charlie said as he helped them through the crowd to the open door of the station's van. "We all thought you were dead."

The concern on their young faces touched Jillian's heart. After her ex-husband and her ex-friend had shattered her trust, she hadn't allowed herself to get close to anyone; she hadn't wanted to care about anyone only to get hurt again. But despite her standoffishness, her coworkers genuinely cared about her. "I'm sorry…"

"For scaring the crap out of us?" Charlie admonished her. "You should be sorry." But then he hugged her, too. "God, Jillian, what the hell happened to you? I saw your car—there's nothing left of it. There was no way anyone could have survived that explosion."

Vicky wiped her face, but tears kept streaming from her eyes. "Do you know how hard it was to report your disappearance? To think you'd been killed…?"

"I'm sorry," she said again with a smile. "But you did great, Vicky."

Charlie gave a vigorous nod of agreement.

"I'm going to have to watch my back," Jillian teased. "You're going to be after my job."

The young woman shuddered. "No, thanks. I don't want to have to get on that side of the camera ever again."

"There are other reporters who could have

covered the story," Jillian pointed out. She wasn't the only on-air talent at the station.

"But it was you…" Her friend swallowed hard. "I'd been talking to you on the phone. Then it went dead, but we didn't want to believe you were—"

"No one else could have reported it," Charlie said, admiration and something else in his eyes as he glanced at Vicky. "At least, they couldn't have done it without trying to steal your job."

Jillian shrugged. "I probably don't have a job, anyway. I'm sure Mike's furious with me."

Charlie laughed. "Are you kidding? You're the only reporter who knows the entire story. You could have a job with any network you want—local or national."

"National," she murmured. It was all she'd thought she'd wanted when she'd started investigating what had been happening around the city. Now she wanted so much more. But Tobias hadn't even looked at her as they'd led him off in handcuffs. Had that kiss just been his way of saying goodbye?

"You're hurt," Vicky said, dabbing at Jillian's lip with a tissue. "Let's get you cleaned up a bit and we'll start filming."

Jillian shook her head. "I can't…"

"You don't look that bad," Charlie said. "I'll use soft focus, low light. 'Course, it would be more dramatic to show your bruises. You took a hell of a beating for this story, Jillian."

"It was worth it," she said, thinking of Tabitha and Tobias. But they weren't together now. The little girl was with social services while Tobias sat in jail. Jillian's head pounded with frustration; she had tried to explain to the police that Tobias hadn't really done anything wrong. The only businesses he'd damaged had been his own. And the man dying had been an accident. They shouldn't hold Tobias responsible for what was all Edward's fault. Either they hadn't understood or they simply hadn't believed her.

"Let's start filming, then," Charlie said.

Jillian shook her head. "I can't."

"You're not ready?" Vicky asked, her eyes warm with sympathy for the ordeal Jillian had endured.

"No. I can't," she explained, "because I promised to keep what I learned off the record."

"But you gave a statement to the police," Vicky said, "or they wouldn't have released you. You would have been held in contempt."

"I told the police so I could help clear Tobias's name," she said. "It wasn't him. It was his twin."

"There are two of them?" Charlie whistled in surprise. "You can't keep a story like this from coming out."

"It will," Vicky agreed. "Just like all those reports about the phantom came out."

"He's not a phantom or a monster." He was the man she loved.

"He's in a lot of trouble," Vicky pointed out. "Not just with the police, but the whole city. Everyone's blaming him. He's facing prison time."

Which meant a longer, maybe even a permanent, separation from Tabitha. Jillian hadn't saved them both only to have them lose each other.

"But I gave my word…" She argued with herself now. Like her, Tobias struggled to trust anyone; she couldn't betray the trust he'd put in her.

She closed her gritty eyes, and like she had before, she saw Tabitha mouthing that plea. *Help me.*

His hand shaking as he gripped the remote, Tobias stabbed the off button. He couldn't bear to see her face, beautiful even with the bruises, as she betrayed him. "She told me it was all off the record," he murmured, his guts twisting with regret. "I should have known better than to trust her."

Nick Morris leaned back in his chair and sighed. The estate destroyed, he'd offered Tobias the use of his house, a small cabin on the wooded outskirts of the city. They sat in the den, which was only big enough for two leather easy chairs and the television console.

"I don't know, man," the security chief said, "she might have just done you a huge favor."

By making him glad he hadn't confided his feelings to her? But he wasn't relieved; he was more than disappointed, too. "What do you mean?"

"We couldn't even get bail until this story started airing," Nick reminded him of his earlier frustration. "Now we're out on our own."

"I wouldn't exactly call this high-tech ankle bracelet 'on our own,'" Tobias said, tugging up his jeans to show off the tracking device.

"Yeah, I've got one, too," Nick reminded him. "But I'd rather wear this than a prison jumpsuit."

"The charges will get dropped," Tobias assured him. "We've got evidence—videos— to prove what he did." Fortunately Edward hadn't figured out that someone had hacked into the security system. He'd revealed more than enough to incriminate himself.

"That footage won't get us off completely," Nick said. "There are other charges. Accessory after the fact, manslaughter…"

"You and I didn't kill anyone," Tobias said. But his gut tightened with regret. "At least, not purposely."

"It wasn't your fault that Hamilton died," Nick assured him. "From the Forces, he had even more experience with explosives than you do. He knew the risks going in."

"But he did it, anyway," Tobias said. "For me."

"For her," Nick said with a smile. "You

know Tabitha has us all twisted around her little finger."

The guys in his unit loved his little girl nearly as much as he did. While all those charges Nick had mentioned were pending, they'd been released, and Tabitha had temporarily been released into his custody. "We'll be cleared." They had to be. He couldn't lose his daughter again. "Or we'll be able to cut a deal for probation." The lawyer they'd hired had served with them, too; he would do everything he could to help.

"Even if we do get cleared," Nick said doubtfully, "there's still the matter of public opinion."

"I don't care what anyone thinks about me." Except his daughter. And Jillian. He had cared what she thought; that was why he'd told her more than he should have trusted her with knowing.

"And Tabitha's custody," Nick continued, as if he hadn't spoken. "You could lose her... if people don't understand why you had to do what you did."

"He was going to kill her," Tobias reminded

him. If not for Jillian, he would have. "He killed those guards and those young women, too."

"Not everyone believes that he's the killer. He looks so much like you…" Nick snorted. "And he's lying through his teeth about everything that happened, swearing that's not him on that footage. That it's you instead. Too bad Ms. Drake didn't shoot him in the heart although I doubt he probably has one."

"I'm glad she didn't kill him," Tobias admitted.

Nick grimaced with disgust and concern. "You don't feel sorry for him…."

"I hate his guts for everything he's done," Tobias assured his friend. "I'm just glad she didn't kill him. She shouldn't have to live with that."

Nick nodded his understanding. "And she saved your life."

"I am grateful for that," Tobias said. "But I asked her to keep everything I told her off the record. I never should have believed her."

Because she'd lied about that, he couldn't trust that she'd had any real feelings for him. Just as his ex had used him for his money and position, Jillian had used him to further her career.

"I know you're crazy about protecting your privacy and all that. But you needed to get your side of the story out there," Nick said. "She did that for you."

"It wasn't her place."

"It wasn't her place to risk her life for Tabitha's, but she did that, too."

Narrowing his eyes in irritation, Tobias glared at his friend. "If I didn't know better, I'd think you had a thing for Ms. Drake."

"I'm not the one with a thing for her," Nick said with a teasing grin. "You're the one who has never missed a single one of her broadcasts."

He gestured toward the blank television screen. "Not anymore."

He would miss Jillian's broadcasts while he tried not to miss her. Even if he could trust her, he had nothing to offer her anymore.

Chapter Sixteen

"It's going to be so weird around here with you gone," Vicky said, spooning the last bite of chocolate cake into her mouth.

Jillian glanced down at the crumbs on her plate, then smiled at her young friend. "You managed just fine without me. You're going to do great."

Vicky shook her head. "I don't belong in front of the camera. And you don't belong here. I can't believe you even had to think about taking the job. It's the national network offer you've been dying to get."

And it was literally almost dying that had put her ambition in perspective for her. Her career was just a job now. She wanted people in her life instead—friends and family. A man to love, a child to cherish…

But since she couldn't have what—or at

least who—she really needed, she would settle for what she'd once thought she had to have.

"Aren't you excited?" Vicky asked as her own eyes sparkled with it. "Your gorgeous face is going to be in every single living room across the nation!"

"Only if they watch the station I'm on," Jillian pointed out with a smile.

"According to the ratings, the majority of viewers will be watching you."

Would Tobias? Or was he too angry to even look at her now? He must have been because he hadn't called. And she hadn't been able to find him. So she'd waited for him to contact her, but the only calls she'd gotten had been job offers.

Too bad that wasn't the kind of offer she wanted anymore.

"Be happy," Vicky urged her.

"Give her a break," Charlie said as he joined them in the break room at the station. "She's been through a lot over the past couple of weeks. She has to process everything."

She hoped he was right—that being overwhelmed was why she dreaded the thought of leaving River City. Of leaving Tobias and Tabitha.

"Any cake left?" Charlie asked hopefully as he glanced around the room.

"Nope," Vicky said as she licked her fork.

"I just wanted another taste," Charlie said, lifting his eyebrows suggestively as he leaned closer to the dark-haired woman.

Glad that two of the people she cared about had found happiness, Jillian smiled as she left them alone. One more broadcast and her packed suitcases would be loaded into a taxi to bring her to the airport. How could she just leave…without seeing him and his little girl at least one last time?

But she had no idea where he was staying. The damaged estate had been boarded up and abandoned. Not a single reporter had been able to reach him for comment about the story she'd told on-air the night he'd been arrested. The night she'd shot a man.

TOBIAS HAD GONE to bed early, hoping he'd sleep right through it. But he couldn't even close his eyes. He stared instead at the dark screen of the television mounted on the bedroom wall of his and Tabitha's new home.

He hadn't wanted to impose on Nick too long and not just because the cabin had been too small for the three of them. Hell, this house wasn't much bigger, but Tobias actually preferred its coziness and warmth to the expanse and elegance of the estate. He preferred its quiet, too—no Nick pushing him to talk to Jillian, or to at least watch her. And remember how much he owed her.

He lifted the remote, his hand shaking, and pointed it at the television. As he turned it on, she lit up the screen with a smile aimed directly into that camera. He felt as if she was looking only at him. His heart shifted with emotion, and he couldn't hear what she was saying for the pounding of his pulse in his ears. But as he reached for the volume button, his door pushed open. He tensed in reaction, ready to fight, then remembered where his twin was—locked up for the rest of his life in a psychiatric hospital for the criminally insane.

A face peered around the side of the door. Wide blue eyes stared at him for a long moment as the little girl studied him. "Daddy?" she asked, her voice quavering with fear and doubt.

"Yes, sweetheart, it's me," he assured her, his heart breaking as it did every time she looked at him with that skeptical expression. "It's me…."

"Daddy," she said with a sigh of relief. Then she threw open the door the rest of the way and ran across the room to vault into bed with him.

"Sweetheart." He wrapped an arm around her thin shoulders and pressed a kiss to the top of her head. "Aren't you supposed to be in your own bed, sleeping?"

She shook her head, her teeth nipping into her bottom lip. "I couldn't sleep, Daddy…."

"Nightmare?" He had brought her to a child psychologist, someone to help her work through the trauma she'd suffered when they'd been apart. The woman had assured him that his just being with her, and loving her, would help her through the worst of her fears. If the district attorney and the judge hadn't agreed to reduce the charges and give him and Nick probation, if Tobias had been separated from his daughter any longer…

Well, he owed Jillian more than his life. Because just as Nick had predicted, her report had changed public opinion—and the judge's—back to his favor.

"I just had to make sure...it was you," Tabitha admitted with a shaky little sigh of relief.

Pain clenched his heart. He hated when she looked at him with such doubt and fear. But, like Jillian, it usually only took her a moment to realize who he was.

"It's me," he promised, pressing another kiss to the top of her head.

"Jilly!" she squealed as she gestured toward the television screen. "It's Jilly."

She'd been asking to see the reporter ever since he'd picked up the little girl from social services. "Yes, it's Jillian."

"Turn it up!" she bossily directed him.

His daughter was coming back to her old self. He smiled and obeyed, pressing the volume button until Jillian's sexy voice filled the room and his senses.

"This is my last night at WXXM," she reported. "After tonight's broadcast, I will be leaving for my new position in New York City."

"No!" Tabitha voiced his protest in a loud wail.

No! he silently exclaimed. She couldn't leave....

But why had he expected her to stay? Even before he had gotten to know her, he'd known she was too talented and too ambitious to be happy for long at a local station.

"Jilly saved me from that bad nanny and the fake daddy," she said. "I need to thank her for helping me. I—I asked other people to help me. The nanny. Some of the guards. But Jilly was the only one who really helped me."

He hadn't. As her father, it was his job to protect her from harm. But he'd failed her. Jillian Drake was the one who'd saved her.

"You *should* thank Jillian," he agreed as he studied the reporter's beautiful face on the flat screen across from his bed. He didn't have to watch her on television, though. He saw her every time he closed his eyes. He saw her as she'd been in his bed, naked and passionate. And he saw her as she'd been when he found her in the warehouse, bruised and bleeding. He finally realized that after what she'd gone through because of him, she deserved to tell the story that had made her career.

She deserved so much more than that,

though. So much more than him. Part of his punishment had been monetary; he had to make restitution for the collateral damage he'd done. He probably wouldn't have much of the ransom left. And he didn't want to work the long hours it would take to amass the fortune he'd destroyed. It didn't matter to him anymore, though.

He should just let her go to the life she'd wanted ever since she'd gotten knocked around in her childhood. Growing up poor and hungry was why Tobias had worked so hard for money and security. But because he understood her so well, he knew that Jillian needed more than career success for true happiness. She needed love.

"Can I make her a pretty thank-you card?" Tabitha asked him.

"You may do that, too. But first you can thank her in person," he said.

Jillian had been so worried about his child that she probably needed to see Tabitha as much as the little girl needed to see Jillian. He shouldn't have kept them apart these past couple of weeks. He realized now that he hadn't avoided her because he didn't trust her, but because he didn't trust himself. He'd never had the best judgment when it came to women. Until now...

Tabitha's eyes brightened with a smile that lit up her whole face. "I can?"

He nodded, his heart filling with love for two females. His daughter. And Jillian. "Let's go."

"Now?" she asked hopefully.

He lifted her from the bed. "Yes."

She gave a delighted squeal as he swung her up in his arms. "But I'm in my pajamas."

"You're perfect."

Jillian would love her. He had no doubt about that. But did she love him enough to stay in River City?

JILLIAN WAITED for the prompt that indicated the end of the commercial break, her attention on the director and the teleprompter, so that she could read the closing remarks of the broadcast. Then she intended to add a few words of her own—a personal goodbye.

A murmur rose up from the crew, distracting her into glancing around the crowded studio. She glimpsed dark hair and broad shoulders, high above everyone else.

Tobias?

People, awestruck as they usually were in his presence, moved aside, out of his way, and she noticed the little girl walking next to him. Tabitha held on to one of his big hands.

"Is that Tobias St. John?" another voice asked, this one coming through her earpiece.

She nodded. Even if she hadn't known that Edward was locked up, she would have never mistaken Tobias for his twin again. "Yes."

"Tobias St. John in our studio?" Mike asked through her earpiece. "Did you know he was coming?"

"No." She had been waiting for two weeks, waiting for him to change his mind and come to her. But all her waiting had been in vain. Until now.

Over the heads of her crew, she met his gaze. Why was he here now…when she was about to leave?

"Jillian, you're on!" the director shouted.

"Make an announcement that a special guest has joined us in the studio," Mike, the producer, urged through her earpiece.

Jillian smiled, but gave a just-perceptible shake of her head. However, her fellow anchor, an ambitious young man, had no such qualms.

"Jillian, look who has come down to the station. The notoriously publicity-shy Tobias St. John." Andrew, the anchor, turned toward the visitor. "Mr. St. John, have you come down to answer some follow-up questions?"

She met Tobias's gaze and offered him an apologetic smile. But he had to know what he had risked coming down to the station during a live broadcast. His privacy. Or had her special report already destroyed that and he had just come down to confront her over running the story despite her promise to keep it off the record?

"I do need to speak to Ms. Drake," he said, his deep voice an ominous rumble.

"Mr. St. John didn't come down here for an interview," Jillian said with a glare at Andrew. She pulled out her earpiece, cutting off Mike's shouted protests.

"No," Tobias agreed. "I'm not here to answer questions. I intend to ask some."

Jillian shivered; he had definitely come down to yell at her. And apparently he didn't mind doing it on-air since he allowed Vicky to attach a microphone to his shirt.

Andrew glanced at her and lifted his brow. Then he turned back to their visitor. "And what are your questions, Mr. St. John?" he asked. "Do you have a problem with the report our own Jillian Drake did about you and your evil twin?"

Jillian glanced at the teleprompter, but it had only the closing remarks for the broadcast. So who was feeding the idiot his lines? Definitely not Vicky.

But no matter how inane the question, Jillian wanted to know the answer. Did he have a problem with her report? Did he feel as betrayed as she'd worried that he would?

His blue-eyed gaze met hers and held. "I did have a problem," Tobias admitted, a muscle twitching along his hard jaw. "But then I realized why she had to share my story with the public."

"Because the public has a right to know," Andrew said, "especially after everything the city went through during those two weeks—with the explosions and the curfew."

Jillian stared at the little girl who clutched her daddy's hand. "It wasn't just the city that went through he…heck," she reminded everyone. "Everything Mr. St. John did, he did to protect his daughter from a psychopathic maniac."

"But Ms. Drake is the one who saved my daughter's life," Tobias said. "And mine." He lifted Tabitha in his arms. "And she wants to say something to Ms. Drake before Jillian leaves the city for her new job."

Static emanated from the audio system as Tobias fumbled with the mike, lifting it toward the little girl's lips. "I—I want to thank Jilly for helping me," Tabitha said.

You're welcome, Jillian mouthed the words, just as the child had mouthed that plea to her a couple of weeks ago.

Tabitha's soft voice cracked with emotion as she added, "She saved me…"

Tobias whispered something in the little girl's ear.

"And my daddy, too," she added with a smile that pulled at the heartstrings of every person in the room.

"Ah, isn't she sweet," Andrew murmured with a trace of bitterness. Apparently, he wasn't as charmed by Tabitha as everyone else was. "But Mr. St. John, you said you had a question for Ms. Drake," the anchor reminded Tobias.

Jillian trembled. He wouldn't yell at her in front of his daughter; he wouldn't want to frighten the child after everything she'd been through. So what was his question…?

Her heart pounded in anticipation. But she didn't want to have this conversation in front of the cameras and the crew. She didn't want to *be* the story. "We're running over," she pointed out, wondering what the heck had happened to the director. "We need to sign off for the night."

"I think everyone wants to know what Mr. St. John wants to ask you," Andrew said.

"Does Ms. Drake?" Tobias asked. "Or am I too late?"

Forgetting the cameras and the crew, Jillian focused only on the man she loved. "Why are you really here? Now…" When she was about to leave…

"My daughter wanted to thank you," he said as he pressed a kiss to Tabitha's temple. "And she's pretty hard to say no to." Tobias walked closer to the broadcast desk until he stood across from Jillian.

"I was going to make you a card," the little girl murmured. He laughed at having his excuse blown.

And Jillian's breath caught at his masculine

beauty. She'd never seen him like this—happy and relaxed. Her heart shifted in her chest as it beat harder with excitement. He wasn't Dante anymore. He'd made it out of hell.

Then he met her gaze again, and his grin faded.

"Why did you really come down here?" she asked.

"I wanted to—I *had* to—see you again."

"You can see me," she reminded him as she tugged off her mike and walked around the desk so that she stood beside him and Tabitha. "All you have to do is turn on your television."

"I had to touch you," he said as he trailed the fingertips of his free hand across her cheek. "I had to kiss you…." His mouth brushed across her lips.

Jillian sighed with pleasure. But he pulled back before either of them could deepen the kiss.

"Daddy!" Tabitha squealed. "You kissed Jilly!"

"Is that okay?"

With wide blue eyes, she looked from him to Jillian and back. Then she gave a solemn nod of approval. "It's great. I think you should marry her."

Jillian gasped. And Tobias laughed again, the sound echoing throughout the studio as everyone watching them laughed, too.

Beneath her dark curls, Tabitha's brow furrowed with confusion. "Daddy, don't you think it's a good idea?"

"I think it's a great idea," he assured her. "But I wanted to do the asking." And there, with the entire viewing audience of River City watching him, he knelt in front of Jillian. "Will you marry me? Will you become my wife and the mother of my child?"

Even though he was on his knees, Jillian wasn't much taller than him. So she was able to stare directly into his eyes, able to see the love in the pale blue depths. No one had ever looked at her like that before; the power of it had tears stinging her eyes and sobs burning in her throat.

"I'm not asking you to give up your new job," he said. "We'll move with you…if you want us in your life."

"I—I want…" she said. "I want to know… why you're proposing." She couldn't just assume what she saw in his eyes was love; she'd been mistaken too many times before to trust her instincts.

"Tell her, Daddy," Tabitha urged him in a loud whisper.

Laughter emanated from the crowd again, but Jillian barely heard them. She was too focused on him.

"I love you," he said, giving her the words she'd needed. "I love you so much that I can't imagine my life without you in it."

"I can't imagine my life without you two," she said. "I accepted that job. I packed my suitcases, but I don't think I really could have left you and Tabitha."

"You really weren't going to leave without saying goodbye?" he asked.

She shook her head. "I couldn't leave you. I love you, too."

A cheer went up from the crowd, but she waved her hand to silence them. Then she turned her attention back to the man she loved. Looping one arm around his neck and the other around the back of the little girl he held, she accepted his proposal. "I will marry you. I will become your wife and

Tabitha's mother and the mother of all the other children we'll have."

She wanted a big family now because she knew, with Tobias, she and her children would be safe. And *loved*.

* * * * *

LARGER-PRINT BOOKS!

GET 2 FREE LARGER-PRINT NOVELS

PLUS 2 FREE GIFTS!

◆HARLEQUIN®

INTRIGUE®

Breathtaking Romantic Suspense

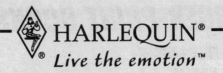

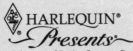

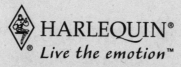

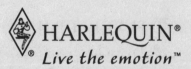

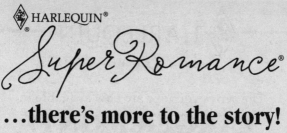

HARLEQUIN®

Super Romance®

...there's more to the story!

Superromance.
A *big* satisfying read about unforgettable
characters. Each month we offer *six* very different
stories that range from family drama to adventure
and mystery, from highly emotional stories to
romantic comedies—and much more! Stories
about people you'll believe in and care about.
Stories too compelling to put down....

Our authors are among today's *best* romance
writers. You'll find familiar names and talented
newcomers. Many of them are award winners—
and you'll see why!

If you want the biggest and best
in romance fiction, you'll get it
from Superromance!

Exciting, Emotional, Unexpected...

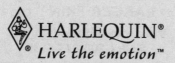

HARLEQUIN®
Live the emotion™

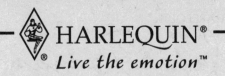

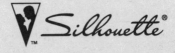